Hair Always Grows Back

ANGELA TANNER

ISBN: 979-8-5494-7903-6

To

Bethany, Ivy, Maddie, and Lydia

ACKNOWLEDGMENTS

Thank you, Laura and Tiffney, for sharing your stories and experiences with me, and for patiently answering my questions.

Thank you to my family and friends for reading and helping me edit this book. Your encouragement and support mean more than you know.

CHAPTER 1

Jojo stood in the middle of the dining room of her new house. She looked around, searching for Ruthie. Where was the little mutt? She knew Ruthie ran in here, and there were only so many places a dog could hide. Then she heard it: the unmistakable sound of a dog's floppy ears slapping against her head as she shook. In the corner of the room was a fake tree and squeezed in behind it was the brown, long-bodied little thief.

"I see you. Now give me back my sock," Jojo said.

Ruthie, sitting behind the tree with the sock in her mouth, blinked at her.

"Ruthie, I see you. Come here."

Ruthie turned her head to face the wall.

"Ruthie! Come here!" Jojo ordered more sternly.

Ruthie squeezed further behind the tree, dropped the sock onto the floor and lay down on it. She let out a loud sigh, glanced at Jojo, then turned her head to face the wall again. She seemed to think that if she couldn't see Jojo, then Jojo couldn't see her either.

Jojo wondered whether she should walk over, grab her sock, and stomp back to her room, or make friends with the miniature dachshund. She really wanted to befriend Ruthie, but she chose to take her sock and stomp back to her room instead. She had learned the hard way that getting attached only led to heartache. Maybe she couldn't choose where she lived, or who she lived with, but she could choose to not get hurt anymore.

Jojo flopped down on the big bed in her new room. She tossed the sock onto the overstuffed chair in the corner. It landed beside its mate on the edge of the seat. Now what? She was home alone because Matt and Amber, her new foster parents, were working at the church across the street. Matt was the pastor of the church, and today he and Amber were setting up tables and things for some kind of special meeting. They had let Jojo choose between going with them or staying home. It was boring staying home alone, especially with no cable tv, but it was better than moving chairs and hearing them thank her for being helpful. She didn't want their praise, or any nice words. She didn't want them to like her, and she didn't want to like them.

Yesterday, her very first day here, Amber had said she appreciated that Jojo had filled up Ruthie's empty water bowl. Jojo had felt bad for the mutt when she saw her licking an empty bowl. But she wouldn't be doing that again. She was determined to keep her distance.

Jojo closed her eyes, suddenly feeling very tired. Since it was a Saturday, she had slept late this morning. Why was she sleepy again? Just then she heard Ruthie running toward her room, her little paws clicking on the wood floor. Before Jojo could stop her, Ruthie grabbed the sock off the chair and ran back out.

"Ruthie!" Jojo yelled. "Come here, you little thief!" She followed the dog through the kitchen and into the family room. Ruthie ran straight under the couch. "Ruthie! Come here!"

She waited, and Ruthie stayed put. She called, and Ruthie ignored her. She pretended to leave the room, and Ruthie sighed and shook her head, her ears making that slapping sound again. Finally, Jojo lay down flat on her belly and looked under the couch. Ruthie's tail end was about six inches from Jojo's face and she was looking back at Jojo, blinking. "I see you. Give me back my sock." Ruthie, sock still in her mouth, again turned her head away. Jojo tried to reach the sock, but she couldn't. She would just let the dog have the sock, except she only had four pairs. Realizing that Ruthie was not going to come out on her own, Jojo grabbed her tail end and gently pulled her backwards. Once she was out from under the couch, Jojo grabbed the end of her sock and tugged. Ruthie, sock still in her mouth, growled and shook her head, enjoying the game. Jojo sat up and tugged again. This time Ruthie surprised her. She let go of the sock, jumped into Jojo's lap, and started frantically licking her face. Jojo knew she should push her off, but she couldn't bring herself to do it. Ruthie was just too sweet. Suddenly Jojo began to cry. She didn't even know why she was crying, but she couldn't stop. Ruthie made a little whimper and gently licked her face, catching her tears.

"I hate it here, Ruthie," she cried. "Sure, this house is okay, but it's not my home. Matt and Amber act all nice, but that won't last. It never does. It's not fair, Ruthie! I just want to go back to my old home." Jojo gently pushed the dog off her lap. No telling how long she'd be here, but she knew she would eventually have to leave, and it hurt too much to get attached again. She considered the family photos that filled the wall above the couch. She didn't recognize any of the people, except for Matt and Amber. The picture of them could have come straight from the cover of a magazine. They were outside on a bright sunny day, sitting on a white porch swing with pots of bright pink and purple flowers hanging behind them. Matt, with his shaved head and blue eyes, was smiling down at Amber. Her wavy light-brown hair was blowing in the wind and she was laughing at something. No, clearly Jojo didn't belong here and, sooner or later, Matt and Amber would figure it out.

Jojo wiped the last tears from her face and carried the sock to her room. This time she put both socks in the black garbage bag lying by her feet. Inside it were the only things that actually belonged to her in this world. She had exactly four changes of clothes, a pair of pajamas, a hairbrush, a toothbrush, and Lamby. Amber had told her she could put her things in the empty dresser and closet, but she didn't do it. Unpacking seemed useless since she would be moving on again soon. Erica, her social worker, had explained that the Morrises were possibly willing to adopt her now that her mother's rights had been terminated. "You're lucky, Jojo," she had said. "You're thirteen years old. Many kids who are as old as you don't get adopted. They end up in group homes. Make a good impression on the Morrises and I think they will adopt you."

She put the garbage bag on the floor beside her and flopped into the overstuffed chair. *There's no use trying,* she thought as more big tears formed in her eyes. *I'll eventually do something they don't like, and they'll get rid of me. I miss my daddy so much! Why did he have to die in that car wreck? Why didn't Mamma love me enough to get off the drugs? Why do I have to be so alone?*

Curling deeper into the chair, Jojo wondered how awful a group home could really be, anyway. At least there she figured she would always know which bed was hers, instead of being sent to different houses, and sleeping in strangers' beds. At least in a group home she wouldn't have to worry about thinking she was finally getting a new family, only to have them tell her they were moving to another state and they decided she was not going with them. Could living in a group home really be worse than living with old Miss

Bonnie, who only spoke to her with demands or mean words? *Will I ever have a real home?* she thought as she cried herself to sleep.

Jojo woke suddenly as a voice called her name. She sat up with a start and found Ruthie in her lap. "What are you doing up here?" she said in a grouchy voice as she nudged her to the floor.

"Jojo," Matt called again from the doorway. "Lunch is ready. Ruthie must really like you. She doesn't usually like new people very well at first." Matt bent down and scratched Ruthie behind her ear. "Did you make a new friend already, Ruthie?" The dog blinked at him and ran to the kitchen. "Well, come on, Jojo."

"I'm not hungry."

"Hey, do you know what you call a fish with two knees?"

Jojo shook her head.

"A two-knee fish!" Matt laughed. Jojo rolled her eyes at him. "Well, come to the table anyway. Two-knee fish! Do you get it?"

She obediently started toward the kitchen, but she did not laugh. Amber set a steaming bowl of homemade chicken noodle soup on the table in front of Jojo, along with a peanut butter and jelly sandwich, and a glass of milk. "I hope you like soup."

Matt joined them at the table and said, "Let's pray."

Jojo wasn't sure what they expected her to do. She had never prayed before. Miss Bonnie, her last foster mother, had taken her to church every Sunday, but they didn't ever talk about God or things like that at home. Matt and Amber bowed their heads, so Jojo did the same. Matt said the prayer out loud while she and Amber listened. "Heavenly Father, thank you for this food You've provided for us. Thank you for sending Jojo to be part of our family. Help her as she adjusts to living in a new home and help us to be a blessing to her. We ask this in Jesus' name, amen."

What does that mean, be a blessing to me? she wondered.

"So Jojo, how do you like your room? Do you need anything?" Matt asked.

"It's fine."

"Do you like chicken noodle soup?" Amber asked.

"It's fine. I'm not hungry."

"Are you sure? You didn't eat much breakfast either. Do you want me to make you something else?

"No, I'm fine." Jojo could see that Amber was concerned about her, but she really didn't feel like eating.

"Erica told us that Jojo is actually a nickname. What's your given name?" Matt asked.

"Joanna Joy, but I like Jojo."

Matt smiled. "I like them both. When I was little, my mom used to call me Matty, short for Matthew. My friends used to tease me relentlessly. I hated that nickname. Now, I just go by Matt, or Pastor Matt."

Jojo took a sip of her milk but didn't say anything else. Amber smiled and asked, "What are your favorite foods?"

"I don't know." She didn't want to reveal too much about herself because she didn't want to get too comfortable here. Besides, giving people knowledge about you was like handing them weapons to use against you when they felt like it.

"If you could pick anything in the world to eat, what would you pick?"

"It doesn't matter."

Matt frowned slightly, "It matters to us, Jojo. We want you to be happy here. We want you to feel like this is your home."

She didn't know what to say to that. This would never be her home. Home is the place where you belong, where there are people who love you and want you to be with them. This place was just the house where she had to live, with people who got paid to keep her.

Amber tried a different question. "What foods do you really hate? Is there anything you really don't like?"

"Anything is fine."

"Fine," Matt said. "You really like that word, I see." Jojo shrugged her shoulders. "Well, do you have any questions for us?" She shrugged her shoulders again.

"I'll just tell you about us anyway then. We have one son, Eli, who is away at college. He'll be home for spring break in a few weeks. He's excited to meet you. You know that I'm the pastor of our church. Amber works as my secretary there. This old house gets pretty quiet with just the two of us and Ruthie, so that's why we wanted you to come and live with us. Plus, after Eli, we prayed God would give us a daughter. Now here you are!"

"I'm not *your* daughter," Jojo said quietly, looking down at her hands. "I already had parents. My dad died, and my mom didn't want me."

"Jojo," Matt waited for her to look up at him, "you're right, you did have parents, but because of situations beyond your control, they aren't here anymore. So, I believe the Lord sent you to us so that you won't be alone in the world. The Bible says that God sets the lonely in families."

"That's right," Amber commented, "We're so glad you're here, Jojo!"

Ruthie put her front paws on Jojo's leg and whined. "Ruthie agrees!" Matt laughed. "Did Ruthie tell you her secret yet?" Ruthie whined again.

"What?" Jojo asked.

"She's going to have puppies in a few weeks!" Amber answered.

"Amber is planning on selling the puppies, but we were thinking that maybe you'd like to keep one. Would you like that?" Matt asked with a big grin on his face.

"Me?" Jojo asked. "I could really keep one?"

"If you'd like," Amber answered.

"I—" Jojo started to say that she'd love to have her own puppy. But what would happen when she had to leave again? "I don't think so. Can I go to my room now?"

Matt and Amber both looked surprised. "You don't want a puppy of your own?" Amber asked.

"No. Can I go now?"

"Uh, sure. Okay," Matt finally answered.

Jojo hurried to her room and shut the door. She curled in the overstuffed chair and looked out the window. It was the middle of March and still winter in this little West Virginia town of Laurel Springs. She could see feathery snowflakes quietly falling. The street was already covered with a thin blanket of bright white snow that made the white siding of the church look dirty. Behind the church, water rushed by in a river that Jojo hadn't noticed before. Snow was starting to settle on the bare branches that hung over the water. She had heard Amber tell Matt that they were predicting two to three inches of snow by morning. Maybe it would keep snowing and they would have a snow day on Monday. She was not looking forward to starting a new school again. Nosy people always asked a bunch of questions that Jojo was tired of trying to answer.

She thought about what Matt had said in his prayer and what he had said to her. Was it possible that God had sent her here on purpose? Did God really do that sort of thing? She had no idea.

She glanced down and saw her garbage bag. She reached inside and pulled out her only friend, Lamby. Miss Bonnie had said she was too old to have a stuffed animal. "Besides, that old, ratty thing is disgusting!" she had insisted. Well, maybe thirteen was too old to have a stuffed animal, and maybe Lamby was a bit worn, but her daddy had given it to her when she was two years old, and Lamby was the only part of her daddy, and her old life, that she had left. She wasn't about to give up Lamby no matter what Miss Bonnie, or anyone, said!

Jojo whispered, "Miss Bonnie thought she got rid of you, but I rescued you. I'll make sure nobody else ever sees you. I'll never leave you, Lamby."

There was a knock on her door. Jojo quickly stuffed Lamby deep inside her garbage bag.

"Jojo, can I come in?" Amber asked quietly.

"Sure," Jojo answered.

"Matt had to go back to the church to study and finish his sermon for tomorrow. I was thinking that maybe you and I could go shopping. Erica said you needed some new clothes."

"It's okay. You don't have to buy me anything."

"I want to! I love shopping. Maybe I should see what outfits you have. Then we can decide what to look for."

Jojo pulled her clothes out of the garbage bag, being careful to keep Lamby hidden in the bottom. Amber sat on the edge of the bed and held up her only long-sleeved shirt. It had a little rip on the side from the time when she had slid into home plate during recess last fall. "Well, you definitely need some warmer things. It's supposed to be close to zero degrees this week. I noticed your jeans look a little big on you. We'll get you some that fit better."

"These used to fit better, but I guess I lost some weight," Jojo commented, looking at her own reflection in the mirror hanging on the back of the closet door. She almost didn't recognize herself. Her brown hair used to be long and silky. Now, it was very short and choppy. Her clothes were about two sizes too big. Her green eyes seemed too large for the rest of her pale face. "I'm not sure what happened."

"Did Miss Bonnie ever buy you new clothes?"

"No, she found these in the free stuff they gave away at her church. She never bought me anything."

"Well, we're going to change that today! Let's go. This will be fun!" Amber stood and led Jojo toward the garage. "Oh, I noticed your jacket is really thin." She handed her a light blue puffer coat. "Here's a warmer coat you can borrow. I'm sure it's too big, but we'll get you one of your own today. Have you been wearing that thin one all winter?"

"I had a warmer one, but I accidentally left it at school one day in January when it was really warm, and it disappeared. I checked the lost and found a lot, but it never turned up. Miss Bonnie said that's what happens when you're irresponsible. She said maybe being cold would make me remember to pay more attention next time."

Amber looked unhappy. She tucked her hair behind her ear and was quiet for a moment. Jojo figured she was probably trying to decide whether or not she should buy new clothes for an irresponsible kid. So, she was a little shocked to hear Amber say, "I think you've had more than enough time to learn that lesson by now. We're getting you a warm coat. Today. And gloves. And a hat."

That night Jojo closed the door to a closet filled with her very own new clothes. She also had new shoes, boots, a thick purple coat with matching gloves, and a hat. She had a dresser drawer filled with new underthings, socks, and two sets of warm pajamas. She carried her new purple toothbrush to the bathroom and placed it in the holder beside Matt's green one and Amber's pink one. It was already getting hard to keep her distance from these people. They were nicer than anyone she had ever known. But that was not necessarily a good thing; it simply made Jojo's situation more complicated.

CHAPTER 2

Jojo awoke Sunday morning at the sound of a knock on her door. "Jojo," Matt called, "Rise and shine! Breakfast is in fifteen minutes."

"Okay," Jojo answered. She raised her arms above her head and stretched. It felt so good to sleep in this big comfy bed. She looked out the window. The ground was covered in a thick blanket of white snow. It made her shiver to think of how cold it was out there. She didn't want to get out of her warm cocoon, so she rolled to her side, pulled the fluffy comforter up to her chin and closed her eyes.

A few minutes later she heard Matt call again. "Jojo, come on. Breakfast is getting cold." She ignored him.

She must have fallen back to sleep because the next thing she knew Amber was opening her door saying, "Jojo, get up. We have to leave for church in twenty minutes."

"I don't want to go."

"Well, I'm sorry, but you have to go."

"I don't feel like going."

"What's wrong? Are you sick?" Amber walked over to the bed and felt her forehead, checking for a fever.

"I'm tired. I just want to stay in bed."

Matt came to the doorway. "Jojo, you have to get up. You can't stay home just because you're tired."

"It's stupid for you to make me go. I'll probably fall asleep during your boring sermon," she snapped.

"Hey, I'll have you know that I'm a funny guy. I'm not boring. Now, let's make like a banana and split."

"Fine," she snapped again. "I'm up." She stomped past him and headed to the bathroom.

Twenty minutes later Jojo and Amber crossed the street and entered the red front doors of the old white church. Matt was already here somewhere. An older couple, both with gray hair, were standing in the foyer. "Good morning, Amber!" the lady greeted enthusiastically. "Who do you have with you today?"

"Good morning, Miss Evie! This is Jojo!" Amber smiled and turned to Jojo. "This is Miss Evie and her husband Mr. John."

Before Jojo could decide what to say, Miss Evie wrapped her arms tight around her in a huge hug. "Oh, it's so good to meet ya, young lady! We've been praying for you!"

Jojo's puzzlement must have shown on her face because Amber explained, "Matt told everyone that you were coming to live with us and asked them to pray for you because we knew it would be difficult to adjust to a new home."

Jojo didn't know what to say to that. "Oh, um, thanks."

Mr. John greeted Jojo with a handshake and a big smile. "Welcome, Jojo. We sure are glad to have ya here."

"Thanks," she said softly.

Amber ushered her into the sanctuary. Besides the lady seated at the piano flipping through a songbook, the large room was empty. They walked up the center aisle and sat in the third row from the front on the left. Amber took off her red wool coat and draped it over the wooden pew in front of them. "I need to grab some things from my office. Would you like to walk with me, or stay here?"

"I'll stay."

"Okay. Sunday School starts in about fifteen minutes. We have an opening time here in the sanctuary, then you'll go to the youth class. More people should be coming in any minute. But, with the snowy roads, we probably won't have a lot of people today. I'll be back shortly."

Jojo was thankful there wouldn't be a lot of people. She felt cold, even though the room was quite warm, so she pulled her new coat tighter around herself. The sanctuary had a high arched ceiling, and large stained-glass windows adorned the walls on either side. In the front, there was a black baby grand piano on the left side of the platform, a wooden podium in the center, and an old pipe organ on the right. The metal pipes were arranged across the back wall of the platform, with another stained-glass window in the center. This beautiful church was very different than the one she went to with Miss Bonnie. It had been very plain, with green carpet and dark walls. No one there had ever said they were happy she was there. As far as she knew, they never prayed for her either.

Why is everyone being so nice to me? she wondered. *What's in it for them?* She thought again about Matt's prayer that they would be a blessing to her. *What is a blessing anyway?*

She could hear voices behind her and knew that people were starting to arrive for Sunday School. She looked down at her hands and hoped that no one would notice her. She heard a lady's voice behind her ask, "Who's sitting in Amber's pew?"

"Oh! That's the young lady Pastor Matt told us about. Her name's Jojo," Miss Evie quickly informed the lady.

"Come on, Lylah," the lady said, "let's go say hi!"

Great. Where's Amber? I don't want to talk to these people.

Without looking up, Jojo could sense people standing beside her in the aisle. "Hi, my name's Lylah. You're Jojo, right?" Jojo looked up and found a girl around her age smiling at her.

"Yes," she answered quietly.

"This is my mom, Michelle."

"Hi, Jojo! It's so nice to meet you! We were hoping you'd be here today," Michelle said, smiling.

"Hi," she responded.

Thankfully Amber returned just then. After a brief conversation, Michelle and Lylah left to find their own seats and Amber sat down beside Jojo. "Lylah is in your Sunday School class. You can walk to class with her in a few minutes."

"Can't I just stay with you today?' Jojo pleaded.

"If you want to, I suppose. You might find the adult class a bit boring though. Wouldn't you rather be with kids your own age?"

"No. I hate meeting new people."

"I'm sorry, Jojo. This all must be pretty overwhelming for you. It will get easier, I promise." Amber's kind eyes and warm smile made her feel a little more comfortable. "You just stick with me and I'll help you get to know everyone."

Sunday School soon began and Jojo didn't have to worry about talking to anyone else. The class lasted for nearly an hour, then there was a short break time before the morning worship service started. True to her word, Amber stayed at Jojo's side the whole time. She introduced her to several people but made sure that Jojo didn't have to say much more than hello to anyone.

Amber was right, the adult Sunday School class had been pretty boring. The teacher was an old man who spoke in a monotone voice. He had some maps and pictures that he showed on a big screen above his head, but Jojo really wasn't interested. The worship service was different though. Jojo enjoyed the beautiful music. The pianist was really talented; the songs were lively. And, she would never admit this to Matt, but he *was* kind of funny. He spoke about some things she had never heard of before. He said that God wants to be our Father, and he wants us to be his children. She had always imagined God to be like a king sitting on a throne, busy doing whatever things a king did. But Matt said that God wants us to talk to him every day, just like we would speak to our earthly father. Her daddy hadn't been a big talker, but he always tucked her in bed at night. Sometimes he would read her a story, and every once in a while, he would tell her a story from when he was a boy. She tried to imagine her daddy wearing a crown and a big royal robe, sitting on the edge of her bed, telling her a story. It seemed pretty ridiculous.

After the service ended, Matt stood in the foyer, just inside the door, shaking hands with the people as they left. Jojo stood quietly beside Amber as she and Miss Evie discussed plans for some upcoming event. From their spot behind the back pew, Jojo watched Matt as he said goodbye to each person. Sometimes he told a corny joke; sometimes he listened intently as a person shared something serious with him. To many people he just said a friendly goodbye, but she noticed that each person left with a smile.

A man in a flannel shirt and suspenders was next in line. Jojo listened to their brief conversation and her heart sank. "Pastor Matt, that's a really good thing you and your missus are doing. Taking in that orphan. That'll show the city council that we do good things here to help this community and they ought to support us. They ought to let us have that lot next door to build a gym."

Matt replied, "I don't know what it will take to convince them to sell it to us. I plan to go see the city planner before the next council meeting. We'll see what he says. You have a good afternoon, Bob."

So that's it. They are trying to impress the city council with their good deeds. That's why they wanted to have me live with them. I guess whenever they get what they want, they'll get rid of me.

When Amber finished her conversation with Miss Evie, she and Jojo returned to the house. Matt would be along as soon as he locked up the church. "Do you like to cook?" Amber asked as they entered the house.

"No, I don't know how to cook."

"Would you like to help me make dinner? I could teach you how to cook."

"No, that's okay." Jojo left the kitchen and headed straight for her room. Ruthie came running in with her, whining for attention. "Go away, Ruthie."

Ruthie ignored the command and jumped up into the chair. She barked and whined and wagged her tail, waiting for Jojo to join her.

"Jojo, please make your bed. Dinner will be ready in about a half hour," Amber called from the kitchen.

It's a waste of time to make a bed. I'm going to be getting right back in it and messing it up again. Actually, that sounds like a good idea right now. She tossed her coat on the foot of the bed and climbed in. Ruthie still stood on the chair whining for attention. "Go away, Ruthie," she mumbled. After a few moments, Ruthie quieted and settled in for a nap herself.

Jojo closed her eyes and thought about all that had happened that morning. Even though she hadn't expected anything better, it still hurt to know that Matt and Amber only wanted to use her to impress some city council. *How generous of them to help the poor little orphan girl. They are such good people,* she thought sarcastically. At first, she considered all the ways she could be a brat and make them sorry for messing with her. She could embarrass them in public or make them super angry. But, in the end, she decided that might actually help their cause because they would look like even more heroic if they were caring for a "troubled" kid. Finally, she decided that the best way to handle the situation was to keep her distance and get it over with quickly. Maybe she could even think of some way to help them get their stupid land so they would send her on her way.

I wonder what God thinks of this. If he really is like a father, is he mad at Matt and Amber for using me? My real daddy wouldn't have let someone treat me like that.

Jojo didn't really fall asleep, but when Amber came to tell her dinner was ready, she pretended not to hear her. Amber stood in the doorway and watched Jojo for a few moments. Finally, Jojo heard her sigh and go back to the kitchen. Jojo smiled to herself and stayed right where she was.

Sometime later Amber returned. "Jojo, it's time to wake up." Jojo didn't move, but this time Amber refused to be ignored. "Jojo, wake up. You've been asleep for almost two hours. You'll never sleep tonight. Besides, Matt and I want you to come to the living room so we can talk."

"I don't want to," Jojo answered.

"Too bad. Come on," Amber said as she pulled the comforter away from Jojo's face.

Jojo sighed loudly. "Fine," she snapped. She stomped into the living room and flopped down on the end of the couch.

"Hey, Sleeping Beauty is awake!" Matt announced. "What did you think of church this morning?"

"It was boring."

The smile on Matt's face faded a little. "Well, at least you didn't say fine." Matt glanced at Amber, and Jojo thought it looked like they were talking to each other with their eyes.

Amber smiled slightly and asked, "Are you hungry? I made you a plate of food and left it on the table. It's probably cold by now, but you can heat it in the microwave whenever you're ready to eat."

Jojo didn't say anything. She didn't really feel that hungry, but she figured she'd better eat something.

"Well, kiddo," Matt said, "we need to talk about some things. First of all, how are you doing? Do you need anything?"

"I'm fine," Jojo answered.

"Of course, you are," Matt said, looking a little frustrated. "Then the next thing is rules and responsibilities."

Great, Jojo thought, *they probably want me to be the maid around here.*

Matt continued, "You are responsible for making your bed every morning and keeping your room clean, doing your homework, and helping with the dishes after dinner."

Matt looked at Jojo like he expected her to say something. *This is so dumb!* she thought but didn't say a word.

"Jojo, did you hear what I said?" Matt asked quietly.

Jojo nodded her head.

"Okay, great. This conversation would be easier if you would talk a little," he said, smiling.

Jojo did not feel like making this easier for them, so she remained silent.

"Fine," Matt said, grinning at her. "It's fine. You just listen and I'll talk."

Jojo could tell he was frustrated with her, but he didn't seem too mad about it. *I wonder what would make him really mad,* she thought. *I wonder what he does when he gets really mad.* She couldn't remember her daddy getting really mad about anything. But her momma sure did. She would yell, and slam doors, and throw whatever was in her hand.

"Amber, can you think of anything I missed?"

"I'd like you to put your dirty clothes in the laundry room. Otherwise, that's it."

"Think you can handle those things, Jojo?" Matt asked.

Jojo nodded.

"Okay, let's talk about the rules then." Matt walked over to the television and picked up the remote. "We don't have cable tv here in rural West Virginia, but we do have internet. So, we have Netflix." He pointed to a button on the remote. "You may watch anytime you want, as long as your other work is finished first. I set the parental controls, so everything should be safe to watch."

That means I probably get to choose between cartoons and nature shows. Perfect.

"What else do you like to do for fun, Jojo?"

She shrugged her shoulders.

"Do you like to read?" Amber asked.

"Sometimes," Jojo answered. She actually loved to read but didn't want to sound too excited.

"Eli loves to read. He has a pretty big book collection in his room. He'll be happy to share them. I'll show you where they are, and you can read as many as you like. I can also take you to the library sometime if you want," Amber said.

Jojo shrugged again.

Matt continued, "You need to be in bed by ten o'clock on school nights. Since you're going to Christian school, I'll be driving you to and from school. We have to leave here by seven-forty in the morning because school starts at eight. I teach first period Bible there to the high schoolers, so we can't be late. Okay?"

This time he said it with her: "Fine."

"At least for now, I'll make your breakfast and pack your lunch. I'll have breakfast ready by seven, so you'll have time to brush your teeth and finish getting ready after you eat," Amber said.

"I think that's everything," Matt said, taking a drink of his coffee.

"Can I go now?" Jojo asked impatiently.

"Come with me," said Amber, "and I'll show you where those books are."

Jojo spent the rest of the afternoon in her room reading. She finally decided she was hungry, so she went quietly into the kitchen to heat up her food, hoping to avoid Matt and Amber. From the kitchen she could see them sitting on the couch. A movie was playing on the tv, but they didn't appear to be watching it. They were talking about the upcoming meeting with the city council.

"I don't know why the city wouldn't want to sell that lot to us," Amber commented. "It's been an eyesore for years. Seems to me they would be glad to have it finally looking nice."

"I know," Matt agreed. "Fred Stanton is just being stubborn. Plus, he's still angry that the council voted to let us close Main Street for the Blueberry Festival last summer. He told Mark Meadows, the new city planner, that if he didn't know better, he'd think this church runs the town."

"Why can't he understand that we want to build a Family Life Center that would provide a place for kids to come after school and in the summer? It's not just for our church kids. This would benefit the entire community."

"I don't know. That's why I want to have a meeting with Mark before the council meeting. I'm hoping to convince him that we are concerned about the kids of this community. If I can make him see that we need the land, I think he can convince the majority of the council to agree."

Jojo's hands started shaking; then her whole body started shaking. She felt like she might be sick. This always happened when she was angry or upset, and sometimes she did throw up. She replayed Matt's words in her mind. "*Trying to convince him that we are concerned about the kids of this community." Well, Matt, you might make the city council believe your lies, but I know the truth. And, as soon as you get the stupid land and send me to a group home, everyone will know you are a fake. I wonder what God will do about that. Does God ever get really angry? Cuz I am angry at him and at his dumb preacher, Matt, and Matt's wife too!*

CHAPTER 3

Monday morning, Jojo found herself in Mrs. Hill's seventh grade homeroom class. Thankfully, her desk was in the third row back on the left, so Jojo slumped down in her seat and rested her head against the wall. This had already been a stressful day and it was only 8:10 in the morning. She had not heard her alarm clock go off, so she was late getting up. While she was glad that Matt and Amber were irritated, she was mad at herself because school was the one thing she really cared about. Most things in her life she couldn't control, but her education was not one of those things. She was determined to learn as much as she could so she could get a scholarship to a good college. One day she would be able to get out of the foster care system and have a happy life.

Cornerstone Christian Academy was not large, but it appeared to Jojo to be a very good school. The building itself looked new; the rooms were bright and clean. The interactive white board at the front of this classroom, and the QR codes posted on the wall, showed they used the latest technology. Jojo had been issued a Chromebook for her personal use. Too bad she wouldn't be staying with Matt and Amber long because she figured she could probably get a good education here.

Everyone she had met so far had been friendly and welcoming. She wished people would stop being nice because it was hard to keep pushing them away. She was determined to not get comfortable here. She glanced around the room and saw Lylah, the girl from church yesterday, sitting a couple rows over. She was laughing at something Mrs. Hill had just said. One good thing about being late this morning was that she hadn't had to talk to any other kids yet. Matt had walked her to her first class and introduced her to Mrs. Hill. She hated making an entrance in front of everyone, but at least she hadn't had to talk to them. Unfortunately, that reprieve didn't last very long.

"Well, gang, we have about ten minutes left until your first period class starts. Why don't you take that time to get to know Jojo a little." Mrs. Hill smiled at Jojo and said, "Our school is not very big really, so you will be with this bunch for all of your classes. They'll show you where to go next."

Everyone turned in their seats to face Jojo. There were several greetings. Jojo wanted to hide under her desk, but she managed a quiet, "Hello."

Lylah pulled on the arm of the boy sitting beside Jojo. "Go talk to Aaron. I want to talk to Jojo." He got up and jokingly shoved her into his seat.

Lylah laughed and said, "Ryan's my cousin. I'm six months older than him, so I'm allowed to boss him around."

"Whatever." Ryan laughed and slid into Lylah's empty seat. "I was planning on coming over here to talk to Aaron anyway."

Ignoring her cousin, Lylah said, "This is Annabeth." The girl sitting in front of Jojo turned around in her seat and smiled.

"Did you just move here?" asked Annabeth.

"Yea," answered Jojo. *And here come the fifty questions. I wish people would just mind their own business.*

"She goes to my church," Lylah added.

"Lylah, what happened to your shirt?" asked Annabeth.

"What do you mean?" Lylah asked, looking down at her blue and purple plaid shirt. Then she spotted the rip on the bottom. "Oh, my goodness!" She laughed. "Sadie, my baby goat, got out this morning. I had to chase her all over the place. When I finally caught her, I had to carry her back to the barn. She didn't like it and kept trying to bite me. Apparently, she got my shirt!"

"She is so cute though! Show Jojo that picture from yesterday," Annabeth said.

Lylah pulled a phone from her backpack and pulled up the picture.

"You're allowed to have phones in school here?" Jojo asked.

"Yea, as long as we don't have them out during class. But if your phone makes a noise in class, or you get caught using it in class, they give you demerits and take your phone for the rest of the day," Annabeth answered.

"Here it is," Lylah said, handing Jojo her phone. The cutest baby goat was standing on top of a car.

"Oh, how cute! How did she get up there?" Jojo asked.

"We have no idea!" Lylah laughed. "She got out yesterday morning and that's where I found her. My dad is going to fix her pen tonight so she can't escape anymore."

The rest of the morning passed quickly. Jojo was pleased to find that people were nice but didn't really bug her to answer questions. Well, everyone except Lylah. That girl could say more words in one minute than Jojo said in an average day. And she was really good at making Jojo talk. Jojo didn't quite know how she did it. Maybe it was because she asked so many questions. After a while it was hard to not answer at least some of them. The thing was, she didn't ask really nosy questions. She asked about Jojo's favorite food, favorite song, favorite everything. She asked if she knew how to ride horses, or how to sew. Lylah also told Jojo all about herself, and all of this happened while still having class! By lunchtime, Jojo figured she knew Lylah better than she knew any other person on the planet.

At lunch, Jojo and Lylah sat with Annabeth, Ryan, and Aaron. The conversation continued much the same as it had throughout the morning.

"Hey, Jojo, do you like to fish?" Aaron asked. "Ryan's dad has a boat and sometimes he takes the four of us out to Cooper's Lake to fish. Maybe you could come with us this summer."

"I've never been fishing before. I wouldn't know what to do," Jojo answered.

"We can teach you!" Lylah offered.

"Or," Annabeth said, "you can just sit with me and watch. Who wants to touch nasty worms and fish? Gross."

"They're not gross!" Lylah insisted.

"I don't know," Jojo said. "I probably won't be here by then. I'm only staying here a little while." *Why did I just say that??? Here come the questions.*

"Oh," Lylah said sadly. "Well, I'm going to pray you're still here then."

No questions? Then it occurred to Jojo that Lylah already knew she was a foster kid. Matt had told the church people she was coming to live with them. *They probably all know. Maybe that's why they haven't been asking the normal questions about where I live and where I came from and all that. Well, maybe that's good. They don't seem to be feeling sorry for me or anything like that.*

"So, what's our next class?" Jojo asked.

"Study hall," Lylah answered. "I have permission to go to the music room to practice piano then. Want to see if Miss Collins will let you come with me, since you don't really have any homework yet?"

"Okay, sure."

The music room was an enormous space with all kinds of band instruments lined up on shelves. There was a black upright piano situated in front of a set of risers. Jojo loved to listen to music, but she knew nothing about singing or playing instruments. Lylah, on the other hand, was a very talented pianist. Jojo sat in a chair beside the piano and watched Lylah's fingers fly over the keys, enjoying the ragtime sounding tune. When she came to the flashy ending, Jojo clapped loudly and said, "Wow! That was awesome!"

Lylah blushed a little and said, "Thanks. That's the piece I'm playing for the fine arts competition next month. I still have some work to do, but it's getting better. Do you play an instrument?"

"No."

"Did you ever want to take lessons?" Lylah asked.

"I never really thought about it. I couldn't even if I wanted to though."

"Why not?"

Stupid, Jojo. Why did I say that? "I just, well," she hesitated, "never had the opportunity."

"I bet Pastor Matt would let you take lessons if you want. He's really nice."

"Yea, right," Jojo mumbled.

"What do you mean?" Lylah asked quietly. "You don't think he's nice?"

"He's—never mind. Forget I said anything."

Lylah was quiet for a moment. "I bet it's hard, coming to live with strangers. Have you had to move a lot?"

"Yea." Jojo started fidgeting with the zipper of her jacket.

"How many times?"

"This is my seventh foster home." Jojo looked up at Lylah and saw shock on her face. She quickly looked back down at her zipper.

"Is that why you said you'd probably be gone by summer? Couldn't you just stay with Pastor Matt and Amber?"

And then, before Jojo could stop them, big tears spilled from her eyes. "It's not up to me, and they don't really want me. Nobody ever does." She looked away and wiped her face with her sleeve.

Lylah turned sideways on the piano bench and placed her hand on Jojo's arm. "That's not true, Jojo. Miss Amber told my mom how excited she was for you to come live with them. She said she'd always wanted a daughter to do girl things with."

"But the thing is, I'm not her daughter. I'm just the orphan they took in so they could impress the city council. They want to buy the empty lot beside the church, and they want the city council to think they are helping the community. What better way to make a good impression than to help some needy kid?" Jojo sniffed and Lylah handed her a tissue. *I shouldn't have said anything. She thinks Matt and Amber are perfect. Now she's probably mad at me.* She grabbed her zipper again and started moving it up and down the bottom of her jacket.

"I really don't think that's true," Lylah said. "Pastor Matt isn't like that."

"You don't know anything about it, Lylah," Jojo insisted bitterly. "I've been in six different foster homes before this. I know how people are. Some are in it for the money, some think it's a noble thing to do. Some maybe do it for the right reason at first, but as soon as something better comes along, they're done. My own momma didn't really want me. Why should anyone else?" *I'm just not the kind of girl a person wants to keep around.*

"What happened with your momma?" Lylah asked. Then she added, "It's okay if you don't want to tell me."

Jojo answered with a sarcastic laugh, "I've already talked to you more than I ever have anyone else. I might as well tell you all of it." She wiped her nose then settled in to tell her story, figuring that Lylah probably wouldn't want anything to do with her after she heard the ugly truth. She might as well finish what she started.

"When I was eight years old, my dad died in a car wreck. My mom and I had a hard time after that. She hadn't ever wanted kids, so I guess I was an accident. And, now that my dad was gone, we had no money and I was just a burden she didn't know what to do with. She started working at a bar down the street from our apartment. Little by little she started drinking. Sometimes she'd come home drunk."

"Who watched you while she worked?" Lylah asked.

"I watched myself. That went on for about two years. Then, one night she just didn't come home. She didn't come home the next day or the next. Finally, a neighbor lady figured out I was alone and called child protective services." To this day Jojo still hated ketchup because that's all she'd had to eat those days: ketchup and crackers.

"They came and took me away. They took me to an emergency foster family. I stayed there for a week. They found my mom sometime that week. She had gone off with some guy and was getting high in a crack house." Thinking about it caused her stomach to churn. She shoved her shaking hands into her jacket pockets.

"Do you really want to hear all this?" Jojo asked Lylah when she realized she was rambling on and on.

"Yes, if you don't mind telling me, I really want to know," Lylah answered softly.

Jojo took a deep breath. "Okay, you asked for it. So next they took me to another house that was supposed to be a more long-term placement. I was there for three weeks. The family had two other foster kids, and the older boy punched me in the face because I ate the last of the cereal. So, they removed me from that house. They sent me back to the first house as another emergency placement. I spent a couple nights there. Then they moved me to the Johnson's house.

"They lived on a farm. Their daughter, Mackenzie, was a real jerk. But they had this sweet barn cat named Callie. I turned eleven while I was living there. They forgot my birthday though. I spent that whole day playing with Callie. By the time Christmas came, they had decided that this wasn't working. The truth was Mackenzie was jealous that I got better grades than her and the teacher liked me. She was used to being the best at everything. So, she got like twenty presents that Christmas. I got one: a new coat. After New Year's, they moved me again.

She pulled her hands back out of her pockets and started nervously shredding the tissue Lylah had given her earlier. "So, this was placement number five. Tom and Debbie Rice were my new foster parents. They were really nice. They had two little boys, a seven-year-old and a three-year-old. They were really cute, especially the little one, Cody. I actually started to like living with them. They treated me like I was part of their family. I still saw my mom once a week then. She was actually doing good for a while. Then she lost her job and started using drugs again. But she said she wanted to get clean so I could come home and live with her, so the judge sent her to a rehab. I was with the Rices for a whole year. A little more than that, actually. Then Tom's job moved him to a new part of the company, which meant they had to move out of state. The judge said I couldn't go because visitation with my mom was supposed to start again the next month. So, that was the end of that". *They said they loved me. But they didn't. They didn't love me or want me bad enough to stay.*

"Next came Miss Bonnie, a mean old lady. Then my mom messed up again and the judge finally terminated her rights. Thankfully, Miss Bonnie didn't want to adopt me, so they took me out of there and here I am."

Jojo ran her hands through her short hair and looked at Lylah. She couldn't tell what the look on Lylah's face meant. Was she feeling sorry for her? She didn't want her pity. *Does she think I'm lying? I should've kept my mouth shut.* Lylah didn't say anything and after a few moments Jojo couldn't take it anymore. "What?"

"I don't know what to say, Jojo," Lylah admitted. "I mean, I'm sorry all that happened to you. But I'm so glad that God brought you here. This means that now you can be adopted, right?"

"Well, yes, but that doesn't matter. Matt and Amber don't want me. I told you that." Jojo gave an exasperated sigh. "This is just temporary. Then I'll get sent to a group home until I turn eighteen. That's just the way it is."

"You're wrong, Jojo. You'll see."

Jojo wasn't going to argue with her about it. She knew the truth.

The rest of the day passed uneventfully. As far as starting a new school went, this time had been the best yet. She was feeling pretty good about the day until she got into Matt's SUV to go home. As soon as she saw him, her insides felt all tense and angry.

"How was your first day?" he asked.

"Fine," he said at the same time she did. She glared at him and didn't say another word.

Later that night, after doing her best to avoid Matt and Amber as much as possible, Jojo climbed into her comfy bed. She hadn't made it that morning since she was running late, but apparently Amber had. This had been a long day but remembering the kids at her new school made her smile. Somehow, Jojo couldn't really explain it, but she felt like a weight had been lifted off her shoulders after telling her story to Lylah. She had never told anyone the things she told Lylah. In fact, she couldn't remember ever telling anyone anything much about herself. She had never had a real friend before. Was that what Lylah had so quickly become? She had a feeling that, besides losing her daddy, leaving Lylah behind was going to be the hardest thing she'd ever have to do.

CHAPTER 4

Tuesday morning started out better than the day before. Jojo woke up with her alarm and was actually feeling hungry. Amber had made homemade pancakes, which Jojo loved. Before they ate, Matt said, "Let's pray."

They sure do a lot of that around here. I'm hungry, hurry up!

"Heavenly Father," he began, "thank you for another day. Thank you for Jojo. Lord, help her to have a good day. Help her to make friends quickly. I'm sure yesterday was tough; being the new kid is never easy. Please help her to know that, even if she feels lonely, that she's never truly alone. You love her and are always with her.

"Please give me wisdom as I meet with the city council this week. Help me be able to convince them that our little town needs this Family Life Center.

"Thank you for this food, and for always meeting our every need. We ask these things in Jesus' name, amen."

That stupid land is all he thinks about. If it was really such a good idea, he wouldn't have to work so hard to convince them. Jojo could feel the anger inside her about to spill over, so she wolfed down her pancakes and left the table without saying a word.

"Jojo," Amber called, "please remember to make your bed."

Not going to happen.

Jojo was ready to leave with a few minutes to spare. She sat on the edge of her unmade bed staring at Ruthie. The dog sat at Jojo's feet staring right back at her. Every once in a while, Ruthie would make a little whine.

"No, I'm not petting you."

Ruthie whined again.

"I don't care how cute you are. I'm not doing it."

The phone rang and Jojo listened through the open doorway as Amber answered it.

"Eli! Hi, son! How are you doing?" There was a pause while Eli was speaking. Then she continued, "Yes, she's all settled in. She started school yesterday."

They must be talking about me. Just like everyone else, always talking about me to social workers and cops and teachers; I'm sick of it!

"I know. She isn't very talkative yet. But that's totally understandable. I just kept praying off and on all yesterday that she'd have a good day. You know, people mean well, but they can ask a lot of questions that I think she'd rather not have to answer. I can't wait for you to meet her! She's been reading some of your books; I told her you would be happy to share them."

She prayed for me all day? Why? I guess it gets her extra points with God.

"Are you ready, Jojo?" Matt called from the kitchen, keeping her from hearing the rest of the phone call.

"Coming," Jojo answered as she grabbed her backpack and walked out of the room, with Ruthie following, whining.

Jojo's second day of school was another good day. This surprised her a lot because this was unlike any other school experience she'd ever had. The people in her class were just nice.

Nobody was mean to anyone else; there wasn't a lot of drama. Unless you counted the moment at lunch when Ryan opened a bottle of Coke that had apparently been shaken. It spewed the sticky liquid all the over the place, which caused everyone to jump back out of their seats. Unfortunately, Annabeth bumped into the kid walking behind her, sending his bowl of red tomato soup flying into the air. Half of the soup landed in Annabeth's hair and the other half landed on the floor, just as another kid came rushing by. He slipped on the wet floor and fell into Jojo, causing her to fall back into her chair. It all happened so fast that the shocked group of kids froze in place for a moment. Then Ryan held up is nearly empty bottle and said, "Cheers!" Everyone erupted in laughter.

Mr. Porter, the science teacher who was on lunch duty, walked over and everyone froze again. He looked at the table full of soggy lunches, Annabeth's dripping hair, the wet floor, and the ceiling splattered with little red dots of soup. He shook his head and said, "I don't even want to know what happened here. Just clean it up."

"Yes, sir," everyone answered.

As soon as he walked away, the laughter erupted again. Jojo couldn't ever remember laughing so hard. Her stomach hurt and tears were streaming down her cheeks. As they worked together to clean up the mess, Jojo felt a sharp pain in her heart because she knew this would all be gone soon.

"Oh, Jojo! Are you okay?" Lylah asked with concern.

"What do you mean? Yes, I'm fine. Why do you ask?"

"You have a big bruise on your arm! You must have fallen really hard!"

Jojo looked down and was surprised by the bruise forming on the side of her arm. "That's weird. It really didn't even hurt. I just fell back in the chair. Maybe I hit it on the side of the table."

"Do you want an ice pack?"

"No, honest, it doesn't even hurt."

"Okay," Lylah said with a frown, as she resumed wiping the table.

That afternoon Jojo walked out the school door with a smile. Then she spotted Matt's SUV and her stomach turned again. How could school be so opposite from home? As she got closer to the vehicle, she realized that Amber was with Matt. She opened the door to the backseat and climbed in, pulling her backpack onto her lap. As she closed the door, she bumped her bruised arm against the backpack. Even though she wore a coat, she could still feel the sting of pain, causing her to wince. Amber turned around just then and saw the look on Jojo's face. "Hi, is something wrong?"

"No, I just bumped into a table at lunch today and got a little bruise. It's nothing."

"Okay, well we need to stop by Mr. John and Miss Evie's for a few minutes. Their furnace quit working today and Matt wants to get it running before it gets too cold in their house. He thinks it's just a pilot light out, so it won't take long. Then we thought we'd go out to dinner. Does that sound okay?"

Jojo started to say it was fine, but she caught Matt smiling at her in the rearview mirror.

"Go ahead and say it, it's…"

"Whatever."

He laughed and pulled out of the parking lot.

Jojo would have waited in the vehicle, but Matt insisted she come inside because it was too cold out, and he didn't know for sure how long it would take. As soon as they walked in the door, Miss

Evie wrapped her arms around Jojo in a big hug. Jojo didn't get hugs from anyone very often, ever actually, so her body stiffened up rigid without her even thinking about it. A hug felt weird. Nice, but weird. After hugging Amber the same way, Miss Evie took their coats and invited them to sit at the kitchen table. She had made hot cocoa and homemade chocolate chip cookies.

"Are you too cold with the heat off?" Miss Evie asked. "I can get ya a sweater."

"No, I'm comfortable," Amber replied.

"Jojo?" Miss Evie asked.

"No, I'm warm enough."

"Well hopefully this hot cocoa will keep us warm." She filled one mug and handed it to Amber. She filled another and handed it to Jojo. When Jojo stretched her arm to accept the mug, her sleeve moved and Amber caught sight of the dark bruise.

"Oh, Jojo! That is a big bruise!"

"What happened, child?" Miss Evie was quick to ask, her voice thick with concern.

"It's nothing. I bumped into the table at lunch today."

"Honey, that looks like more than a bump," Amber worried.

"Truly, it didn't even hurt when it happened. I don't know why it made such a big bruise."

"You must've hit it at a bad angle or somethin'," Miss Evie concluded. "Do you need some ice to put on it?'

"No, it's fine. I promise."

Apparently satisfied, Miss Evie passed the plate of cookies to Jojo and changed the subject. "Has Ruthie had her pups yet?"

"Soon!" Amber answered excitedly. "Sometimes I can see her little belly moving around! It's the sweetest thing. I can't wait to see them."

"Are ya gonna keep any of 'em?'

Amber glanced at Jojo, then back to Miss Evie. "We haven't decided yet."

I decided already. I'm not going to fall in love with a sweet little puppy, then have to leave it. I had to leave Callie. I'm not doing that again.

"Are you and Mr. John going to take a puppy? You know I'd give you one in a heartbeat."

"Oh, not us. Mercy! We're too old to be chasin' after a pup."

"Heat's back on. Now, who you callin' old, Evie?" Mr. John asked, as he and Matt came back up from the basement.

"I'm callin' you old!"

"Well, you'd better speak for your own self. When Pastor Matt gets that Family Life Center up and runnin', I'm gonna go down there and play ball with those young'uns. I've still got some spunk left in me."

"What do you think about it, John? Do you think the council will agree to sell the lot to us for a reasonable price?" Matt asked.

"It's hard to guess. I don't know why they wouldn't, but people are odd critters sometimes. Ya just never know. Are you gonna speak at the meeting on Thursday?"

"I'm going to, but I'm not totally sure what I'm going to say. Got any advice for me?"

"Well, just find a way to show them we care about the kids of this town. That shouldn't be too hard. I mean, look at you two. Obviously, you care about kids, anybody with two eyes can see that."

"I hope that's what they see."

Jojo slurped her cocoa, using the rim of the mug to hide her scowl. *You sure don't want them to see the truth, do you? Now, we're going out to dinner. Is that so you can show off your little orphan girl? I'm glad the meeting is this week. I'm so sick of this. Let's just get it over with.*

By the time that Thursday evening came, Jojo was sick of reading in her room, so she was sitting on the couch watching a movie with Amber when Matt came home. Amber paused the movie and asked, "How did it go, honey?"

"They voted no, four to three against."

"Seriously?" Amber questioned, her voice rising slightly.

"I am." He sat down and leaned his head against the back of the chair. "Fred Stanton was obviously a no. I stopped in to see Mark Meadows earlier this afternoon, and he wasn't very optimistic it would pass. He told me that Fred plays golf with the other three guys a lot. He said that Fred and his buddies filed paperwork to turn that lot into overflow parking for the library."

"Overflow parking for the library?" Amber said indignantly. "That's ridiculous! When has the library's parking lot ever been more than half full?"

"I know, Amber, that's exactly what I asked," he replied with equal frustration. "Mark didn't have an answer. He said he's new, so he doesn't have much influence with the city council."

"Can we appeal their decision? We've worked too hard to give up now!" Amber folded her arms and her neck flushed red with irritation.

"I don't know." Matt stood up crossed the room to look out the window, with narrowed eyes and a deep scowl.

Jojo began to worry what he would do next. Would he start yelling and throwing things? Should she be afraid of him? *Are you a monster, like Brent, when you get angry?* She could clearly remember the night she accidentally spilled her momma's beer. He'd thrown the empty bottle across the room, and it shattered against the wall. Then he'd grabbed Jojo by the hair and made her pick up the broken glass with her bare hands. Her momma had just sat in the corner crying the whole time.

Matt turned back to look at Amber and Jojo. "This is so frustrating!" he said loudly. "I have tried everything I can possibly think of to persuade them." He shoved his hands roughly into the pocket of his pants and turned back to the window.

After a quiet moment, Jojo released the breath she didn't realize she'd been holding. Maybe he wasn't going to explode after all. Then his words from a moment before echoed in her mind again. *"I have tried everything I can possibly think of to persuade them." You must want that land awfully bad to get a foster kid to prove your point. Too bad your little scheme didn't work. Now what?*

Then Matt calmly said, "I guess it's all been for nothing."

"Serves you right," Jojo mumbled.

Matt and Amber both turned to Jojo with looks of surprise. "What's that supposed to mean?" Matt asked, sounding offended.

"Nothing," Jojo snapped.

"No, why would you say that to me?" he demanded.

Jojo snapped to her feet. "Because I know what you did!" She started to storm out of the room.

"Stop!" he ordered loudly. She froze in place. He lowered his voice and said, "Jojo, please, come back. I have no idea what you're talking about. What did I do?"

Amber stood to her feet, looking flushed and upset, as Jojo turned around and answered, "I heard you talking to that man at church. I know you just took me, this poor orphan girl, so you could convince the city council to give you your precious land."

Matt was speechless for a moment. Jojo stared straight into his eyes, daring him to deny it.

"Oh, Jojo," Matt's voice broke as if he were almost ready to cry. "Sweetheart, that land is not *precious* to me. *You* are. Our reasons for wanting to adopt you have absolutely nothing to do with a piece of land."

"Not even a little bit, Jojo," Amber added.

"I heard you!" Jojo yelled, as tears rolled down her face. "I heard that man say that it was such a good thing you and the missus were doing, taking in an orphan girl! He said that ought to convince the city to give you the land! I heard you!"

"What did you hear me say, Jojo?" Matt said loud enough to be heard over Jojo's last words. Then more quietly he asked again, "What did you actually hear *me* say?"

Jojo was shaking with anger and hurt. "You told him that you didn't know what it would take. Just now, you said that you did *everything* you could possibly think of!"

"Not that, Jojo. I would *never* think to do that." Matt rubbed his hand down his face. "You don't know us very well yet, but I promise you that we would never use you to get a piece of land or to impress anyone."

Jojo took a deep breath, trying to stop her hands from shaking. *Is he being honest? What is happening?*

"I know it's early yet, but we already know we want you to be part of our family," Amber said softly. She gently placed her fingers on Jojo's cheek and turned Jojo's face to look into her eyes. "We want this to be your forever home."

My forever home? Could this possibly be real, or was this some horrible trick? Will they send me away now that they lost the land? They seem like they mean the things they said, but so did the Rices. How could she ever know the difference between lies and the truth?

"That's what we want, Jojo. What do you want?" asked Matt.

Jojo looked back at Matt, trying to comprehend what they were saying, what they were asking. She was so confused. *What do I want? No-one ever asks me that. I just get hauled about here and there like a package.* Finally, she whispered, "I don't know."

Matt wiped a tear from his own eye and laughed. "You've only been here six days! I guess it's pretty reasonable that you don't know what to think of us yet. We should probably give you until at least next week!" He grinned and wiped a tear from Jojo's face. "It's going to be okay, sweet girl."

Amber wrapped her arms around Jojo and kissed the top of her head. "We have all the time in the world to get to know each other. It's going to take some time, but eventually you'll learn to trust us. I'm sure of it!"

"It's getting really late," Matt realized. "You need to get to bed. Are you okay?"

Was she okay? Jojo had no idea, but she nodded anyway.

"Good-night," Matt and Amber both said.

Jojo whispered, "Good-night." Her head pounded as she laid it on her pillow. *What do I want? I don't know. What's the point of wanting things that you can never have?*

CHAPTER 5

Amber stuck her head around Jojo's partially open bedroom door.

What does she want now? Did I forget to do a chore? Jojo wondered, raising her head without smiling.

"Jojo, I think it's time for Ruthie to have her puppies! Want to come watch with me?"

"Sure, I guess" Jojo answered. She put her Chromebook on her bed and followed Amber to the garage. She wondered what this would be like. *No big deal,* she told herself.

"Have you ever seen puppies be born before?" Amber asked quietly, as they sat on the step outside the kitchen door. Ruthie was in a big box in the corner that had her food and water bowls and a big thick blanket.

"No, I've never seen anything be born before."

"It's amazing to see a new life come into this world! We'll stay over here and just keep an eye on her. I don't want to disturb her if we don't have to. This is her second litter. She was such a good little momma the first time."

Did Momma get this happy when I was born? I guess not. Maybe Daddy did though… even if he hadn't planned on being a dad. It must be nice to have people hoping and praying for you to be born, getting ready to celebrate the big event. Jojo felt herself tensing up so she picked at a fingernail and then asked, "How long will it take?"

"Well, the vet said she's having three puppies this time. So, probably an hour or two. She had four the first time and it took about two hours."

"What did you do with those puppies?" Jojo asked.

"I gave one to my sister, Megan. Then we sold the other three. I had planned to keep one, but a teacher at your school really wanted one."

"Will you keep one of these?"

"Well, that's up to you," Amber said with a little smile.

Jojo didn't say anything. These last few weeks had been so confusing. One minute she was angry at Matt or Amber, and sometimes she didn't even know why. Then, other times, she began to feel like maybe this could become a real home. Trust was a hard thing for Jojo to do. She didn't trust Matt and Amber to not give up on her. She also didn't trust herself. Just last night, Matt had brought her home a bag of orange gumdrops, her absolute favorite treat. She still had no idea how he found out they were her favorite, or how he found a whole bag of only orange ones! Part of her wanted to tell him thanks and give him a big hug. Nobody had ever done something that nice for her. But then, she began to doubt his motives. Was he just doing this to impress someone? She was starting to see that he really wasn't trying to do that. But, if that wasn't the reason they were being nice to her, what was the reason?

For the next two hours, Jojo watched Ruthie, and sometimes Amber, care for these tiny new puppies. They were adorable! Amber had been right, watching a new life come into the world was amazing! Sometime during the process, Matt joined them. He pulled an upturned bucket over beside Amber and sat on it.

"Two boys and a girl," he proclaimed. "What should we name them?"

"Hmmm, I don't know," Amber answered.

"Won't their new owners want to name them?" Jojo asked.

"Yes, I'm sure they will. But I like to give them names while they're here."

"How about Nina, Pinta, and Santa Maria," Matt suggested.

Jojo laughed. "Which boy would be called Nina?"

"Oh, my goodness," Amber said, laughing with her.

"Good point," Matt conceded. "Okay, I got it, Rock, Paper, Scissors."

"No!" they answered, giggling.

"Bacon, Lettuce, and Tomato?"

"You'd better leave the naming to us," Amber said

"I agree," Jojo added.

"Fine," Matt said, winking at Jojo. "I'm going to go make dinner."

Jojo couldn't help but laugh. That had been her favorite word for a while.

"Wait," Amber said, "since when do you know how to cook?"

"Who said anything about cooking?" he said, pulling out his cell phone. "I'm going to *make* a phone call. Pizza or Chinese?"

"Jojo?"

"Um, pizza sounds good," she answered.

"I'm on it. Dinner will be ready in about thirty minutes," he said and disappeared into the kitchen.

"He's crazy sometimes," Amber said, smiling, "but I sure do love him. So, what are we going to name these little guys?"

"We could name the boys Tucker and Boone, and the girl Minnie, short for Mineral," Jojo offered.

"You've been studying West Virginia geography, I see. I love it!"

"So which boy is which?" Jojo asked.

"I think we should call the light brown one Tucker and the dark brown one Boone," Amber decided.

"I can't wait to hold one," Jojo said.

"I'm going to clean things up a bit. If you'll help me, we'll go eat, and then come back and do just that."

Later that evening, Jojo sat on the floor with Amber, playing with the new puppies. Ruthie lay nearby watching and resting, while Boone slept beside her. "You were right," Jojo said, "watching a new life come into the world was pretty amazing."

Amber smiled. "It's a miracle for sure. Did you ever have a pet of your own?"

Jojo stroked the head of little Minnie. "No, not really. There was this sweet cat, named Callie, at one of my other foster homes. But she was just a barn cat; she didn't belong to me."

"I like cats too, but Matt hates them. It's because he's allergic to them. One time we visited an older lady who used to go to our church. We didn't know it at first, but she had like five or six cats living in her tiny house. We hadn't been inside for more than five minutes when I looked over and saw Matt. His eyes were nearly swollen shut. He started sneezing and sneezing and sneezing. I bet he sneezed over a hundred times before we got home. I felt bad for him, but it was a little funny too because he kept trying to talk and sneeze at the same time." She put Tucker back in the box with Ruthie, and Jojo did the same with Minnie. "Still today, if you want to get him riled up, just tell him you want a kitten for a pet," she giggled.

"I'll have to remember that," Jojo said.

Amber pulled her knees up and wrapped her arms around them. "So, you still don't think you'd like to have a puppy of your own?"

Jojo decided to be honest. "It's not that I wouldn't love to have one. The problem is having to leave it behind. I still miss Callie, and I only had her for a few months, and she wasn't really even mine."

"And it hurts too much to say good-bye," Amber said, showing she understood.

Jojo nodded but didn't say anything.

"I can understand that, Jojo. Maybe, in time, you will feel more certain about the future. You know, your social worker, Erica, came by earlier today while you were still at school. We had a nice talk about you."

"What's new?" Jojo blurted out, sounding madder than she meant to. *Now I've gone and spoiled my time with Amber and the puppies. But I don't like everyone talking about me, again!*

Amber ignored Jojo's tone of voice. She nudged Jojo with her arm. "No, seriously, it was a great conversation. She asked how we thought you were doing. I told her that she needed to get your perspective, but we think you seem to be adjusting well. We told her how much we love having you here, and that our hope is to adopt you. But we told her we would not consider doing that unless that's what you wanted. And, Jojo," she waited until Jojo looked at her, "it's okay if that's not what you want. As long as you're happy here, we can continue just the way we are. Erica agreed that we could continue to just be your foster parents."

"Why do you want to adopt me?" Jojo asked. She just couldn't understand it.

"Oh, Jojo, that's easy to answer! We love you!"

"But you didn't even know me until a month ago."

"You're right. But we had been praying for you long before that. Matt and I had always wanted another child, but for reasons only God knows, that didn't happen. We had talked and prayed off and on about adopting a baby, but it just never seemed like the right time. Then a few months back, we felt like the Lord was telling us now was the time. Looking back, I believe that's because He knew you needed us, and we needed you.

"So, we started praying that He would send us the child that would complete our family. Then, once we had completed all the training and the home study, it was finally time. We got a call from Erica telling us about you, and we knew you were the one God was sending to us."

"But what if you didn't even like me?"

Amber laughed. "Well, I suppose that could have happened, but as soon as I saw you, I knew."

"Knew what?"

"That I would grow to love you as my own daughter."

"I'm not even very nice a lot of the time," Jojo muttered. A heavy weight seemed to be pressing the words from her chest through her tight throat.

"True story!" Amber laughed again. "No, honey, you can be moody now and then, but who isn't? None of us is perfect. And do you know what? Love isn't just nice feelings. Love is a choice. I choose to love you, even on the not-so-good days, and all the nice feelings just fall into place. I guess that sounds kind of silly, doesn't it?"

"Kind of," Jojo agreed, puzzled. *She sure is different than Momma and that mean old Miss Bonnie I lived with.*

"Maybe this will help explain what I mean. Do you remember the day you met Lylah?"

"Yes, my first Sunday here, at church."

"Right, and did you look at her that first day and think she would become your best friend?"

"No, I didn't want to talk to her."

"Exactly. But, once you got to know her better, what happened?"

"She became my best friend."

"Would you say you love her?"

Jojo gulped. Love was a word that made her feel weird; sort of like she was a shy little animal wandering down a quiet road when a big car came roaring up at her. It made her want to jump and run. "Well, I guess I *like* Lylah."

"Okay," Amber continued, "so what would happen if Lylah had a bad day and was really grouchy towards you? Would that liking go away?"

"It's hard to imagine her doing that, but, no, she would still be my best friend."

"And that, Jojo, is how we feel about you!"

Jojo wasn't sure what to say. *Maybe they do plan to keep me. Is it really possible that they won't send me away? Do they love me?* Jojo rubbed her head behind her ear. The ache was starting to get worse.

Amber noticed and asked, "What's the matter? Is your head hurting?"

Jojo nodded, "And my ear. It started this morning."

"Oh, you should've said something." Amber felt her forehead and said, "You feel very warm. Come with me, and I'll get you some medicine."

Jojo followed her into the kitchen and Amber took her temperature. She did have a fever. She took two Ibuprofen, then

Amber said, "Why don't you go get ready for bed. I'll be there in a minute with something to help your ear feel better."

A few minutes later, Jojo was dressed in her pajamas and sitting on the edge of her bed. Amber brought in a glass jelly jar filled with warm water and a towel. She sat beside Jojo and pulled a pillow onto her lap. "Come here, lay your head on this pillow and I'll hold this warm jar on your ear for a few minutes. The heat might help the pain a little."

Jojo rested her head in Amber's lap and closed her eyes. Amber gently ran her fingers through Jojo's short hair. It felt so good. She couldn't remember anyone ever caring for her like this. "I used to have long hair," she commented.

"You did?"

"Yea, it was so long I would accidentally sit on the ends of it sometimes."

"Wow! That was really long. Do you like your short hair better?"

"No, I hate it actually." Jojo could still remember the way the long silky strands would glide through her fingers. She opened her eyes and studied her reflection in the mirror that was on the back of the closet door. Now the short choppy hairs curled on the ends and stuck out everywhere.

"So, what made you decide to get it cut short?" Amber asked

Jojo could feel the anger building up inside her just thinking about it, making her whole body tense. "I cut it myself." Disgusted with the sight of her hair, she closed her eyes again and tried to relax. Amber continued to gently run her fingers through Jojo's hair, and didn't say anything so Jojo continued, "Miss Bonnie always yelled that I didn't get it clean, and I didn't get all the tangles out. So, every night, she used to make me sit while she brushed my hair, like I was a little kid or something. She would use this scratchy brush and would pull hard. It hurt really bad! So, one night, I refused to let her brush it. She got so angry. There was a lot of yelling, then finally she grabbed my arm and marched me to my room. I slammed the door in her face, and she said I wasn't going to school until I cooperated."

Jojo found Amber's eyes in the mirror trying to see her reaction. She couldn't tell. Amber readjusted the jar to put more warmth on Jojo's ear, but still didn't speak. Closing her eyes again, Jojo blurted out the rest. "That night, I decided I wasn't going to let her pull my hair ever again. I wasn't going to let her win. I waited until she was asleep, went down to the kitchen, and found the scissors. I cut it so short there wasn't enough left to get tangled anymore."

Amber was quiet for another moment, then she smiled and said, "I can teach you how to get all the tangles out by yourself."

So, she's not going to take Miss Bonnie's side and tell me how wrong I was for cutting it? Jojo wasn't expecting that. "Did you forget? My hair is too short to get any tangles now."

"It will grow. If you want, I can take you to my hairdresser. She can trim the ends and show you how to style it as it grows out."

Jojo suddenly felt like she had a huge lump in her throat. She sat up and said, "You mean, I could have *pretty* hair again?"

"Jojo, your hair is beautiful now! I love your little curls." Standing, Amber motioned her under the covers. When Jojo was settled in her bed, Amber touched a little brown lock of Jojo's hair. "But you absolutely can have long hair again. That's the best part about hair; it always grows back!"

Hair always grows back! That's true! Jojo smiled and realized her ear did feel a little better.

Matt knocked on the door frame. "Can I come in?"

"Sure."

Amber moved over and he sat on the edge of Jojo's bed. "I'm sorry you're not feeling very well. Can I get you anything?"

"No, thanks. I'm—" realizing what she was about to say, she giggled, and he said it with her, "fine."

Matt shook his head and tousled her hair. "You are really warm," he noted with a frown.

"My head and ear are hurting, but it's getting a little better." She looked at Amber, "Thanks for taking care of me."

"You're welcome, sweetheart." She put her hand on Matt's shoulder and said, "We'd better let her get some rest."

"Let's pray first." He took Jojo's hand in his and bowed his head. "Heavenly Father, please help Jojo to get the rest she needs tonight, and for her to be feeling better quickly. And, thank you for allowing Ruthie's puppies to arrive safely. We love you, Lord, amen."

Matt stood and kissed the top of Jojo's head, "Good-night. Let us know if you need something."

"I'll check on you before I go to bed," Amber assured her. "Good-night."

The next morning Jojo was still running a fever, so Amber took her to the doctor. Turned out to be an ear infection. The doctor gave her an antibiotic, and she was feeling much better in a few days. But the memory of the way Matt and Amber had taken care of her was something she wouldn't soon forget.

The week after Easter was spring break for Jojo, and for Eli. Matt and Amber had been bragging about him for days. He was captain of the swim team, and a straight A student. According to them, he was pretty much perfect. *What if he doesn't like me and wants them to get rid of me? What if he's a jerk?* Her mind was constantly worrying about all the different possibilities. She was dreading his arrival so much, that it was actually a strange relief when the day finally came.

He got home on Friday afternoon. Amber rushed out the door when she heard his car pull in the driveway. Matt looked at Jojo, who was sitting on the floor holding Tucker, and said excitedly, "Come and meet Eli!"

She placed the puppy back in the box with his siblings and stood up. *Well, here goes nothing.* Taking a deep breath, she followed Matt into the kitchen.

Eli and Amber were just coming through the door as Jojo came into the room. "Hey, Dad! Long time, no see." He hugged his dad, then looked behind Matt and straight at Jojo. She was so nervous; the palms of her hands began to sweat. Immediately Eli smiled warmly and said, "Hi, Jojo!"

"Hi," she answered shyly.

They decided to go to the park and have a picnic for dinner. It was unusually warm for late April, nearly eighty degrees. Surprisingly, Jojo liked Eli right away. He was tall and handsome and funny, like his dad. He asked a lot of questions, like Lylah, but not about really personal things. Eli told Jojo that he'd always wanted a baby sister to pick on, and seeing as how she was already thirteen, he had a lot of time to make up for.

She quickly pointed out that she technically wasn't his sister at all.

"I never get stuck on technicalities," he answered, and stuck a piece of ice down the back of her shirt. She squealed and chased him around the picnic table. She stopped on one side, and he stopped on the other, waiting for her to make her next move. Matt gave her a cheesy grin and handed her an open bottle of water.

"Hey," Eli complained, "I saw that."

"I knew those eyeglasses would come in handy someday," Matt said.

"Eli!" a voice called from behind him. He turned toward the person coming his way. Jojo seized the opportunity and climbed up on the picnic bench. Just as the guy made it over to where Eli was standing, she started to pour the water on Eli's head. He jerked around and grabbed her wrist as she hopped off the bench. He took the bottle and emptied the last bit on her. They were both laughing as he introduced her to his friend Josh.

"Josh, we just finished eating," Amber said. "Are you hungry? There's plenty left?"

"No, thanks. My dad grilled steaks earlier."

"Well, we're going to walk down to the lake. Want to join us?" she asked.

"Sure, sounds good."

"You guys start walking that way," Matt said. "I'll go put this stuff in the vehicle and catch up to you in a minute." He picked up the cooler in both hands and headed towards the parking lot.

"You need help, Dad?" Eli offered.

"No," Matt answered, turning back. "It's not heavy."

"I need to tie my shoe real fast," Jojo said, sitting down on the bench.

"Dad!" Eli yelled and started running toward Matt.

Jojo turned around to see Matt lying flat on his back, the cooler thrown to the side.

She, Amber, and Josh headed in the same direction as Matt sat up. "I'm okay," he said, laughing. Eli helped him to his feet.

"What happened?" Amber asked.

"I don't know," he answered. "I slipped on something." He paused for a moment and scrunched up his nose. "What is that *smell*?"

Josh, who was now standing behind Matt, burst out laughing. "It's dog poop!"

Eli was laughing hysterically too. "Man, that had to have come from a *big* dog! Dad, your whole back is covered!"

"Nasty!" Matt said, clearly disgusted. He tried to look over his shoulder at the back of his shirt. "The stink is enough to make me throw up. What kind of idiot leaves their dog's poop in a park?"

Jojo stopped giggling and watched Matt carefully. Was he going to kick anything, or yell at passersby? She glanced at Amber but Amber didn't look worried; she was still laughing. Jojo's rigid body began to relax.

"My backpack's in the SUV," Eli said, still laughing. "Give me your keys and I'll get you a clean shirt."

Amber, going between laughing and trying to hold her breath to keep from inhaling the stink, helped Matt get the soiled shirt off without touching his head.

Jojo stood back, watching the scene before her. Her mind suddenly flashed back to the time Brent had stepped in dog poop on the sidewalk in front of her old house. A stray dog had just finished his business and was taking a drink from a puddle. Brent had been furious. He walked over and kicked the dog as hard as he could. The force knocked the poor dog off its feet, and it slid to the middle of the street. It yelped and tried to limp away. Jojo had been horrified. Then Brent ripped of his soiled boot and threw it at the dog with all his might. Thinking about it still made Jojo's stomach hurt.

A man came rushing over, a large black and white dog at his side. "I'm so sorry!" the man said. "Frowzy decided to do his business right there a few minutes ago. I just went back to my truck to get stuff to clean it up."

"Frowzy, huh?" Matt said. "Doesn't that mean foul-smelling?"

"Uh, yea," the man grinned.

"I'd say that's the most accurate dog name I've ever heard," Matt laughed.

"Are you hurt?" the man asked.

"No, I'm not hurt. No harm done. I'm Matt Morris," he said offering his hand.

"Jeff Underwood," he said, shaking Matt's hand.

"Good to meet you," Matt said, smiling.

Jojo still stood by herself, watching. After his conversation ended and he had changed his shirt, he walked over to her. "What are you thinking, kiddo? You're awfully quiet."

"Are you sure you're okay?" she asked

"I'm *fine*," he said putting an arm around her shoulders. "Let's take that walk."

Jojo enjoyed the rest of the evening very much. They walked down to a beautiful lake, and Eli and Josh taught her how to play the game of horseshoes. The whole time she thought about how different Matt was from Brent. Maybe her future was brighter than she realized. *As long as they don't change their minds about me. I haven't done anything really bad yet… would they still love me then, and want me?*

CHAPTER 6

Jojo was getting ready to take a shower Saturday morning when she realized she had a big bruise on top of her hand and wrist. *What in the world? I don't remember doing anything to cause this.* She rubbed her wrist with the opposite hand and noticed another bruise on her leg. After a closer examination, she found four more bruises on her body. She thought it was odd, but didn't know what to do about it, so she jumped in the shower and finished getting ready. Amber was taking her to the hair salon today. Hopefully the lady could do something about her unruly mop.

While sitting in the waiting area of the salon, Amber was flipping through a magazine of short hair styles and asking Jojo what she thought about some of them. As Jojo pointed to one picture to say she liked it, Amber saw the bruise on her wrist. "Jojo, what happened?" Her voice was filled with concern as she pushed up Jojo's sleeve to get a better look.

"I don't know," Jojo answered. "I don't remember hurting myself."

"Wait, is this where Eli grabbed you yesterday when you were pouring water on him?"

"Um," Jojo thought for a moment. "Yea, I guess it was this hand. But it didn't hurt at all. He didn't hurt me."

Amber's voice rose slightly in alarm. "Jojo, people don't get bruises like this without something causing it."

Amber looked worried, and Jojo didn't like it. *I hope she doesn't make a big deal about this. I like Eli. I don't want him to be mad at me already.* Thankfully the stylist called her name just then, so she hoped that was the end of it.

It wasn't. Jojo was sitting on the porch swing later that evening, sort of reading a book. For some reason she couldn't seem to focus on the story; she kept dozing off. Eli came out the front door looking for her.

"There you are. Scoot over, kid." She made room for him and closed her book. "Mom said you have a big bruise on your wrist from where I grabbed you yesterday. I'm really sorry! I sure didn't mean to hurt you!"

They were talking about her behind her back again. *I wish they would stop doing that!* Jojo thought he looked genuinely sorry. "It's okay, Eli. I guess I just bruise easily for some reason. It didn't hurt, I promise." She really didn't want him to feel guilty. She knew all too well how a guy as big as Eli could hurt her if he wanted to. And she knew he hadn't done anything wrong.

"Still, I promise to be more careful from now on." He leaned back and started moving the swing back and forth. "What are you reading?"

She showed him the cover of the book. "Honestly, I can't seem to get into the story," she said. "I'm kind of tired."

"That's a good series. You should keep reading it when you're more awake. You'll like it. So, how do you like it here? Mom and Dad treating you okay?"

That's a good question. Do I like it here?

"It's okay. They're not too bad most of the time."

"They sure do like having you here. I can tell you that." He smiled and said, "Mom loves having another girl around."

"That's what they say anyway."

"You don't believe them?" Eli asked sounding more curious than accusing.

"I've learned that adults are really good at saying stuff to get you to do what they want. It doesn't mean it's real or that they'll keep their word."

Jojo immediately thought back to the time her foster parents told her they were planning a real vacation to the beach. She had always dreamed of seeing the ocean and feeling the sand between her toes. They had said if she did all her chores and proved she could be good, that she would get to go with them. She had done everything they said, but they didn't keep their promise. A few days before they were supposed to leave, the lady called Erica and told her they didn't feel comfortable taking Jojo with them so she needed to find a temporary place for her to stay until they got back.

"Humm, that's sad, Jojo." He frowned. "I can tell you from experience though, that my mom and dad are not like that. They say what they mean and mean what they say." He laughed a little and continued, "Sometimes I wish that wasn't always the case."

"What do you mean? You wish they would lie to you?"

"Well, not lie exactly, but sometimes I wish they didn't always keep their word. For example, when I was about your age, I went through this stage where I hated getting up early and getting ready for school. Part of that was because I was staying up late playing a video game, but they still don't know that. So, don't tell them. Anyway, Dad had told me that if I made him late for school one more time, I wasn't playing in my next basketball game. Well, we made it to the championship and the Friday before the big game, I didn't get up on time again so ..."

"Seriously? He wouldn't let you play?" Jojo was astonished.

"He's a man of his word." Eli smiled. "Boy, was I angry at the time. But, you know, looking back, I'm glad he didn't let me play."

"No, you're not." Jojo couldn't believe it. "Why would you be glad?"

"Because I always knew I could trust him to keep his word. I still can. Besides, I deserved it."

"I guess that makes sense, in a twisted sort of way," Jojo conceded.

"There's Josh," Eli said as a gray truck pulled into the driveway. "See ya later, kid."

Matt and Amber keep saying they want me. God, if you're really there, would you please not let me get hurt anymore? Maybe I do want to stay here.

Easter, or Resurrection Sunday, as Matt liked to call it, was a big deal. Jojo found it hard to drag herself out of bed, as usual, but the bright sunshine streaming through her bedroom window, and the smell of frying bacon, made her want to get up. She put on the flowy yellow dress that she had picked out yesterday when Amber took her shopping. She put on her matching sandals and took extra time with her hair. It was definitely starting to grow but was still short. The stylist had evened it out yesterday and showed her how to fix it, so it looked cute. And, even though she had cut a little off, it actually looked longer when she straightened the curls out. She studied her reflection in the mirror. *This is as good as it's going to get, I guess.* She could hear Eli and Matt laughing in the kitchen and decided to join them. As she entered, Matt and Eli both stopped laughing and looked at her.

"Look at you!" Matt said, smiling. "You look beautiful this morning, Jojo!"

Jojo looked down at her feet and said quietly, "Thanks." *I hate this awkward stuff.*

Amber turned from the stove and smiled. "You do look very pretty, Jojo. Breakfast will be ready in a few minutes."

"Go see what's in your Easter basket," Eli said. "I guess they think I'm too old. I didn't get one."

"I can exchange that gas card for a basket with bubbles and a plastic dump truck like we gave you when you were little, if you want," Matt said holding out his hand.

"That's okay, I'll pass," Eli answered. "Come on, Jojo, let's see what you got."

Jojo walked over to the table and stared at the first Easter basket she'd had since she was eight years old. This one was a beautiful white basket with a big lavender bow tied on the side. It was so perfect looking, Jojo almost didn't want to move anything inside it. Almost. *This is the prettiest gift I've ever been given.* She carefully began to lift the items from the basket. There were chocolate eggs and jellybeans, and another bag of orange gumdrops. "How did you know these are my favorite?"

Matt shrugged but didn't answer.

She looked back inside the basket and couldn't believe what she saw. Underneath the bag of gumdrops, was a box that had a picture of an iPhone on the top. She gasped. "Is this-?"

"It is," Matt confirmed. "But it's a gift that comes with some conditions. Okay?"

Like what? It gets taken away if they change their minds? Jojo waited for him to explain before answering.

"Amber and I were thinking that you would probably enjoy being able to text your friends and things. But it stays on the charger in our room after ten on school nights and eleven on weekends. We have parental controls set, so some things are definitely limited." Jojo nodded, figuring that wasn't so bad. "And, we will be checking your phone frequently. We want you to enjoy it, but more importantly, we want to keep you safe."

So, they are basically going to be spying on me. Great.

Eli seemed to know what she'd been thinking because he nudged her shoulder with his own and said, "Hey, you don't have any secret crimes to hide anyway, right? So, it's not such a big deal." He looked straight into her eyes, commanding her attention. "It's. A. Phone," he whispered.

It is a phone. My very own phone. "You're right," she whispered back. Turning to Matt, she said, "Okay, I guess I can live with that." She looked down at the phone in her hand and smiled. *My very own phone!*

She looked around and an overwhelming feeling of joy came over her in a way she had never experienced before. It almost didn't feel real. She was standing in the middle of a sunlit kitchen, with people who not only said they wanted her, but who proved they meant it by doing nice things for her all the time. As she looked at their faces, thoughts and memories of her days here all began to flood her mind. They cared enough to buy her the things she needed, but also things they knew would make her happy, like orange gumdrops. They cared enough about her to set rules and make sure she followed them. They cared for her when she was sick. They played games with her. They encouraged her. They laughed with her. They protected her. They prayed for her.

Then, before she even thought about what she was doing, she rushed over to Matt and hugged him; and he hugged her right back. She almost did not stiffen inside his arms. He kissed the top of her head and said, "That's the best thank you I've had in a long time."

She turned and hugged Amber too.

"Okay," Matt announced before things could get too awkward. "We're going to be late for church if we don't get moving. You guys go ahead and eat breakfast, I've got to get to the church. See ya shortly."

Jojo walked into the youth Sunday school room and found Lylah already sitting in their usual spot at the long table. "Your hair looks awesome! Did you get it cut yesterday?"

"Yes, and Debbie, the stylist, showed me how to fix it so it looks better. I'm going to grow it out. Guess what! I got a new phone for Easter!" She pulled her new phone out of her pocket and showed it to Lylah.

"Awesome! Plus, I love this case with flowers on it! What's your number and I'll text you mine?"

They spent the next several minutes playing with their phones and taking Easter selfies.

"So, what did you get for Easter?" Jojo asked.

"I'm getting a new saddle, but it won't be here until later this week." Lylah loved her horses and various other farm animals. "When it comes in, will you come riding with me? You can use my old saddle. It's still good. My new one is better for jumping. I'm hoping to start competing by next year!"

"I don't know how to ride a horse."

"That's what you've got me for! I'll teach you."

"It sounds fun, and also a little scary," Jojo admitted with a laugh.

"Nothing to be afraid of, you'll see. Speaking of being afraid though," she lowered her voice, "I'm worried I failed the math test we took on Thursday. If I did, my dad's going to kill me."

"I could help you study next time, if you want," Jojo offered. "I'm usually pretty good at math."

"You're good at everything," Lylah huffed.

Jojo wasn't sure what she meant by that. *Is she mad that I'm good at math or that I offered to help her?* She wasn't sure how to respond, so she looked at her hands and picked at a fingernail.

"I'm sorry, I didn't mean to sound like I'm mad at you or anything," Lylah said. "It's just so depressing that I work so hard and can't get it, and you don't seem to have to work at all."

"I do have to work some, but you're right, math is usually pretty easy for me. But I could never begin to play piano like you do, or sing, or jump horses. Life would be pretty boring if we were all good at the same things. Right?"

"I suppose so," Lylah grudgingly agreed.

"Maybe God knew what he was doing, making us all different."

"You said that like you meant it, Jojo. Do you believe God is real? I thought you said before that you didn't."

Lylah was right, she had said that. When did that change? She wasn't sure when it happened, but she knew it had. "I didn't realize it until right now. But, yes, I do believe in God."

"Yay! What changed your mind?" Lylah asked, clearly excited.

"I don't know exactly. I have seen God answer prayers too many times lately for it to be a coincidence. But it's more than that. I don't know how to explain it, but I believe it."

"What prayers have you seen answered?"

"Several. At the mall one day, it was pouring rain, and Amber quickly said, 'Lord, please give us an empty parking spot close to the door' and he did. Matt prayed for Ruthie's puppies to be born safely, and they were. He prayed it would be sunny today, and it is. And, I think one of the biggest ones is they prayed that I would have a good first day of school and that I would make friends quickly. That has never happened before." Jojo smiled to herself. *God, maybe you really did send me here on purpose. It sure seems that way!*

Jojo was still feeling very happy as she and Amber walked home after church. As she looked down the street, she could see the empty lot beside the church. It was all grown over, and there were little purple wildflowers growing along the sidewalk. She thought it was a bit ironic that something as nice as the little flowers could grow in the middle of such an ugly mess. The red brick library sat on the other side of the lot. Across from the library sign were pots overflowing with vibrant pink and red flowers hanging from the lamppost on the edge of the sidewalk. Jojo crossed the wide street toward the house, thinking about how she loved all the bright colors of spring. She was carrying a second Easter basket. Mr. John and Miss Evie had made it for her. She couldn't believe it! She could see that it was filled with candy and some more of those tasty homemade cookies that Miss Evie was so good at making. Amber, who was ahead of her, opened the front door and a puppy ran out and straight down the steps. Jojo tried to grab him, but as she turned around, her foot slipped off the step, causing her to lose her balance, and she landed on her bottom. "Oh, Jojo! Are you alright?" Amber asked rushing toward her.

"Yea, but grab Tucker before he runs into the street!"

Amber started after the puppy, but he ran straight across the street and Eli caught him. She turned back to Jojo and helped her gather the spilled contents of the basket. "How did he get out of his crate? I'm sure I locked them in before we left."

"I don't know, but he sure is fast!"

They stood and headed up the few steps to the porch. "Are you okay? Oh, Jojo," Amber said as she looked at the back of Jojo's legs. "You have more bruises starting. I'm going to call the doctor tomorrow and get you an appointment for a checkup. Maybe you have an iron deficiency or something."

They headed inside to round up the other puppies. Eli brought Tucker in and placed him in the cardboard box with Ruthie. Jojo brought the basket into the kitchen, placed it, and her phone on the table, and called for the puppies. Amber found Minnie in the bathroom, shredding a roll of toilet paper. "No, Minnie," she scolded. She sounded stern, but Jojo giggled as she watched her scoop up the puppy and kiss her nose before she settled her in the crook of her arm.

"Uh oh," Eli called, "I found Boone. He's in Jojo's room and it looks like he's ruined something."

Jojo stood in the doorway of her bedroom, frozen in place. She could see little bits of white cottonlike stuffing covering the entire floor. The pillows were still on the bed where she'd left them. There was only one other thing in this room she could think of that would have white fluffy stuffing. Then she spotted the little pink bow lying beside the open closet door. She shook her head in disbelief as tears rolled down her face. "No," she cried. "No, please no!"

"Honey, it's okay," Amber said, wrapping an arm around Jojo. "Whatever it was, we'll replace it. Don't cry, sweetheart."

Amber handed Minnie to Eli so she could wrap her arms tightly around Jojo. "What was it, Jojo? Why are you so upset?"

Sobs shook her body, and all Jojo could answer was, "Lamby. My Lamby is gone."

CHAPTER 7

Amber eventually led Jojo into the family room and sat on the couch with her. After a long while, Jojo's tears dried up and she fell asleep with her head on Amber's lap. She awoke sometime later and found Amber was gone. Her head was resting on a pillow and someone had covered her with a thin blanket. As the memory of her precious Lamby in shreds on her bedroom floor returned, her tears began quietly falling again. *God, how could you let this happen? I wish I never would have come here.*

"You're awake," Amber said softly as she entered the room. Jojo sat up and wiped at her tears with her hands. Amber handed her a tissue. "I'm so sorry, Jojo. Please tell me about your Lamby. I've never seen her before."

She wiped her eyes with the tissue as Amber sat beside her. "My daddy gave her to me on my second birthday. She was the only thing I had left of him. Now Lamby is gone. They're gone."

"I'm so sorry, Jojo," Amber said again as she wrapped her in another big hug. Jojo's body was tense and stiff.

"Me too," Jojo said harshly. "I wish I never would have come here. Then I'd still have my Lamby."

Amber let her go and didn't say anything else. Her eyes looked troubled. *I probably hurt her feelings,* Jojo thought. *But what about MY feelings? No-one knows how my heart feels like it's being shredded into tiny bits, just like Lamby.*

Jojo leaned away from Amber and pushed her face into the sofa cushions.

Maybe Amber understood that Jojo needed some space. She stood up, but before she left the room, she asked, "Are you hungry?" When Jojo didn't respond, she continued, "I made you a plate. It's sitting on the stove. Matt and Eli had to run an errand. They'll be back in a little while. I'll be in my room if you need me."

Jojo waited until Amber disappeared before she stood and went to her own room. Someone had cleaned up her floor. Lamby, all the little bits of her, was gone. She closed the door and crawled under her covers to cry some more. *I know Amber didn't mean to let the puppies get out, and I know this is not really her fault. But God, you could have stopped this from happening. I can't believe that the exact day I realized you're real, is the day you broke my heart. I thought you were supposed to be good. Well, you're not. I hate you!*

"Jojo, can we come in?" Matt called.

"What for?" Jojo asked grumpily.

"We need to show you something."

"I guess," she answered sitting up. *Why did I say yes?*

Matt opened the door and he, Amber, and Eli came into her room. Amber sat on the edge of her bed and handed her a heart-shaped pillow. "I know it's not the same, but we gathered up all the pieces of Lamby and I sewed them inside this heart."

"My Lamby's in here?"

"Yes, she's in there," Amber answered as she wiped tears from her own eyes.

"Thank you," Jojo whispered, too overwhelmed to say anything else.

Matt cleared his throat and said, "We have something else to give you."

Eli handed her a gift bag with bright flowers all over it. She held her heart pillow in one hand and pulled the yellow tissue paper out of the bag with the other. Inside was a snow-white teddy bear, with a light pink bow tied around its neck.

Matt continued, "We were thinking that if it was okay with you, Amber could take some of the stuffing out of this bear and sew your Lamby safely inside. That way, you would have something from your daddy and from us."

She looked at the bear and back to each of them. As the idea began to sink in, she realized that she loved it.

"Would that be okay, Jojo?" Amber asked.

She nodded, "I think that would be really nice."

Eli chuckled and everyone looked at him to see what was so funny. "I guess it's kind of perfect that your Lamby gets resurrected on the same day we celebrate Jesus's resurrection."

"That's one way to look at it, I guess," Matt said laughing. "I don't know about you guys, but I'm starving. Let's go find some leftovers and decide what we're going to do all week. It is spring break after all."

While driving to the local greenhouse Monday morning, Jojo listened as Amber used the speakerphone to make an appointment for her with Dr. Heather Lindsay. They were going to pick out some flowers and strawberry plants to put in pots on the front porch. The receptionist said that Dr. Lindsay was on vacation for the next several days, but if it was urgent, they could see Dr. Camden right away.

Amber glanced at Jojo, who was shaking her head. Amber had explained earlier that Dr. Camden was an older gentleman, who had been Eli's pediatrician for many years. "No, I don't think it's that urgent," Amber explained. "She has some unusual bruising and fatigue, but no other symptoms really. I'm wondering if she is lacking in a particular vitamin or something. We'll wait to see Dr. Lindsay. I think Jojo would feel more comfortable with a lady."

"Then I can schedule you for a week from Thursday, at two. Will that work?" asked the receptionist.

"Perfect," Amber answered.

They pulled into the parking lot of a huge nursery. There were green plants and flowers spilling from hanging baskets, barrels, and shelves underneath the covered storefront. Jojo looked around, admiring all the bright colors and varieties. They headed to a large fenced in area to the left of the building. Amber grabbed one of the special carts designed to hold plants and they started shopping. Jojo had never planted anything before, but she thought she might really enjoy this. There was one area that had a little pond surrounded with decorative rocks and greenery. There were live fish swimming around lily pads. She pulled out her phone and snapped a picture, thinking she'd love to have something like that of her own someday.

After they finished their shopping, Amber announced she was ready for lunch. "We haven't taken you to Rowdy's yet, have we?"

"No," Jojo answered, "but Lylah says they have really good milkshakes."

"Oh! She's so right! You're going to love it."

Rowdy's, a burger place that looked like an old barn, was crowded with people. They chose to sit in the outdoor seating area. The tables were made of rough wood and covered with green umbrellas. Upbeat country music filled the air with a fun energy. Jojo ordered a cheeseburger, fries, and an orange cream milkshake. The burger and fries were great, but the milkshake, topped with homemade whipped cream and orange flavored drizzle, was amazing!

She texted Lylah, telling her she finally had a Rowdy's milkshake and sent a picture of her delicious treat. Lylah texted back that her new saddle wasn't going to be here until next week, but her mom was going to call Amber and see if they could come for a cookout later today. *That would be so much better! I'll get to see Lylah's house and her animals, maybe even pet a horse. But I won't have to ride one!*

That evening Jojo carried a tray of brownies, that she had made, and placed them on the picnic table in Lylah's backyard. Lylah came running over and excitedly hugged Jojo. "I'm so glad you guys could come! Did you make the brownies? I love brownies!"

"Yes," Jojo answered proudly. "I did make them. Cracking open eggs without getting pieces of the shell stuck in it, is not a talent I have." She giggled. "Thankfully, Amber told me to break them in a little bowl before I put them in the mix. Otherwise they might have been a little crunchy."

"Come on, let's go see the horses. I want to introduce you to Rio and Rain. Dad is just now putting the chicken on the grill. It's going to be a while before we eat," Lylah said leading her towards the barn.

"Don't you just love that smell!" Lylah said dreamily as the girls stepped inside the barn door.

Uh, she can't be smelling the same stink that I smell. "You love this manure smell?" Jojo asked, wrinkling her nose.

"Okay, maybe it's not the same as brownies or something, but it's not so bad. It's not really manure, it's just the smell of barn," she answered, giggling. "You'll get used to it."

Lylah reached out her hand and rubbed the side of a tall brown horse's neck and face. "This is Rio," she said as he tilted his head into her hand.

"Aw," said Jojo. "He must think that feels good."

"He loves to be petted. You can pet him."

"Will he bite me?"

Lylah giggled, "No, he would never do that. Would ya, Rio?" He sighed and tilted his head toward Lylah's hand again.

Jojo tentatively reached up her hand and softly touched the horse's neck with the tips of her fingers. She could feel strength in his muscles as he turned his head to face her. She took a step back.

"It's okay," Lylah reassured her. "Here, hold your hand out flat and give him this." She dropped a sugar cube into Jojo's hand. "You give him that, and he'll be your best friend forever."

The horse's tongue tickled Jojo's hand as he quickly found the sweet treat. Then he lowered his head, trying to reach Lylah's hand for more. "No more," she said laughing. He kept trying to get his big muzzle into her little jacket pocket.

"He's pretty smart; he knows just where you keep those," Jojo commented.

"No, Rio," Lylah tried to say in a sterner voice, while continuing to laugh. "He's something alright!"

They moved on to the next stall where Lylah introduced her to Rain, a black Quarter horse. "That's an unusual name," Jojo commented. "What made you decide to call her Rain?"

Her official name is Rain Dancer. She was already named when we got her."

"I really like it," Jojo said thoughtfully. She's beautiful. I can imagine her dancing in an open field with thunder and lightning and pouring rain."

"Oh, that reminds me of something I want to show you. Come on."

Lylah led her up a ladder into the hayloft. The sweet fragrance of the hay and the warm sunlight flooding through the open hay door was a pleasant change from the stall area below. They walked over to the open door and sat down on the soft hay. "You can see almost all of our property from up here," Lylah explained. "See that pond over there?" she asked, pointing to the far right. "My grandparents live on the other side of those woods that are beyond the pond. I ride Rain over there all the time.

"The goats are over there. The babies are in that pen," she said pointing to a fenced off area beside the barn.

"Is that the same river that runs behind the church?" Jojo asked, pointing to the left.

"Yep. If you got in the river there, you would eventually end up here."

"It's so peaceful up here," Jojo said quietly.

"They say West Virginia is almost heaven," Lylah said. "I think maybe that's true. Of course, I haven't really been to many other places, but I think God made an awfully pretty place for us to live."

God again. Something had really been bugging Jojo lately, and she figured maybe Lylah would have an answer. She picked up a piece of hay and started breaking it into little pieces until she got up the courage to ask, "Lylah, if God is real, why does he allow bad things to happen?"

Lylah turned to look at her, "What do you mean?"

"He let my dad die. He let me have to go to all kinds of crummy foster homes. He even let one of the puppies destroy the one thing I had left of my old life. If he really does love me like everyone says, why did he let all that bad stuff happen?"

Lylah looked back out the door and was silent for a moment before answering, "God is real. I don't completely understand why he lets some things happen. Pastor Matt says that God doesn't do things *to* us. He does things *for* us. I don't believe it's his will for bad stuff to happen, but because we have a free will, he allows it to happen sometimes."

"That doesn't seem very loving to me," Jojo said.

Turning back to Jojo, she said, "I think the thing is not why he allows something to happen, but what he does when bad things happen. We may never know why something happens until we get to Heaven. But, look at how God carries us through the bad stuff when we ask him."

Jojo thought about that for a moment. "I don't know if I really understand what you mean."

"Well, you said how bad your life was before, but look where God brought you now. Isn't this better?" Lylah asked.

"It's way better! This is the first real home I've ever had since my dad died," Jojo realized how true that was as she said it. "I wonder sometimes if it's too good to be true. What if they get sick of having me around?" That bit of doubt came creeping back again.

"That's not going to happen." Lylah laughed. "What did you mean about one of the puppies destroying the last part of your old life? What was it?"

She's probably going to laugh at me. "You'll probably think it's silly, but I had this little stuffed lamb that my daddy gave me on my second birthday. It was really worn out. I kept it in a bag in my closet."

"I don't think that's silly. I still have a stuffed giraffe that my grandad gave me for Christmas when I was little. If you put batteries in it, it laughs." Lylah giggled. "I still love that thing. I keep it on my bed."

"Really?" Jojo asked, feeling relieved that she wasn't the only kid her age with a stuffed animal.

"Sure, and I have a box full of teddy bears in the back of my closet. I gave some away a few years ago, but I kept all the ones I really like."

"Well, Boone chewed my Lamby to shreds." Jojo had to blink fast to keep tears from forming now as she thought about it again.

"Oh, Jojo, I'm sorry!" Lylah said.

"It's okay. Actually, it turned out to be better than I imagined it could."

"How?"

"Amber took all the little bits of my Lamby and sewed them inside of a little heart-shaped pillow that she made. Then, they got me a new white teddy bear and she took some of the stuffing out of it and sewed the heart inside the bear."

"So, now you have something from your first family and your last family!" Lylah said, grinning.

My last family? God, could that really happen? Or are you going to break my heart again?

"It sounds like that's another way that God was taking care of you in spite of a bad situation, right?"

Jojo considered that for a moment. "I suppose it's possible. But why would he not just protect my Lamby in the first place? He knows how important she is to me. Why would he break my heart like that?"

"Have you and Amber taken the puppies for their first vet visit yet?" Lylah asked.

Jojo shook her head, confused by her sudden change of topic. "Not yet, but what does that have to do with God letting my Lamby get destroyed?"

Ignoring Jojo's question, Lylah continued, "When you do take them, the vet will have to give them their first shots, right?"

Deciding to just wait and see where she was going with this, Jojo agreed, "Yes."

"Do you think those puppies are going to understand what's happening to them? I mean, all they are going to know is that you and Amber, the ones who supposedly care for them, are letting some mean guy poke them with a needle. It's going to hurt."

"Okay," Jojo said, still quite confused.

"You and Amber will help hold those puppies while the vet gives them shots, even though you know it's gonna hurt. Right?" Jojo nodded. Lylah continued, "Exactly, and you'll do it because you know that it's what's best for them. Those puppies are never going to understand it, even when they grow up. But because you love them, you'll put them through a little bit of pain now so that they won't get rabies or some other really bad sickness later on. See what I mean?"

Jojo picked up some more hay. "Are you saying God let my Lamby get destroyed because he thought it was best for me?" *How could that possibly be what's best for me?*

Lylah shrugged. "I don't know. I'm not God."

Could losing my Lamby somehow be what's best for me? Jojo knew she was going to have to spend some time thinking about that. But Lylah's mom, Michelle, called for them to come and eat. That thinking would have to wait for another time.

Lylah practically flew down the ladder. Jojo followed much more carefully. She really didn't feel very hungry, but Lylah appeared to be starving the way she rushed toward the table. Jojo never felt like rushing anywhere anymore. For some reason she always seemed tired. Maybe Doctor Lindsay would have some magic pill that would make her feel better. But that was another thing she would have to think about later. For now, she was going to enjoy hanging out with her best friend, and she was going to eat one of the first brownies she had ever made, even if she didn't feel hungry.

CHAPTER 8

Spring break seemed to fly by. Eli returned to college for his last few weeks of classes, and Jojo had to start back to school herself. Unfortunately, on the third day, she overslept again. She had been late twice this week already, and it was only Wednesday. She rushed to dress and brush her teeth.

"We have to leave in five minutes, Jojo," Matt called from the kitchen. She could hear the annoyance in his voice.

She was so mad at herself. She had wanted to spend extra time making her hair look nice this morning, and here she was just trying to make it lie flat. Ruthie wandered into her room as she threw her hairbrush on her unmade bed. *Amber's not going to like that, but I can't help it. I don't have time today.* She had been trying to follow the rules and be good. She figured they were trying to be nice to her, so she should try to do what they asked her to. Well, most of the time. She hated doing the dishes, so she usually found some excuse not to help do them. If she was doing schoolwork, they pretty much left her alone about the dishes, so she always made it a point to work slow enough to still have something to do after dinner.

Ruthie whined for attention, but Jojo ignored her. She and Ruthie had become pretty good friends lately, but Jojo didn't have time for playing this morning. Amber hadn't said anything else about

Jojo keeping one of the puppies. But if she brought it up again, Jojo had decided to say yes. She had also decided that, as long as they were willing to keep her, she wanted to stay. It was just different here. It felt like home.

"Jojo! We have to go!"

"Coming," she called grabbing her backpack. *I hate being late.*

Her day did not get better as it went on. By second period she had already managed to make Annabeth mad because she told her to mind her own business. Annabeth was just trying to be nice, asking why she was in such a bad mood today. Then Mrs. Williams, their English teacher, had given her demerits for texting an apology to Annabeth during class, but thankfully hadn't actually taken her phone.

Fourth period science class was the class that finally did her in. Somehow, she had completely forgotten about the test. She never did that. *How did this happen? I cannot afford to fail this test, but I am totally not prepared. What am I going to do?*

Jojo could feel the tension building inside her. There had to be something she could do. As Mr. Porter handed her the test, an idea popped into her head. She looked over the test and began to do the questions that she knew the answers to. Mr. Porter sat down at his desk and began to work on paperwork.

Jojo took off her jacket and placed it on top of her desk, partially covering her test. She glanced around and determined that everyone seemed to be focused on their own test. Mr. Porter continued to work. She slowly slid her phone out of her jacket pocket and hid it under the edge of her jacket. She found the picture she was searching for. It was a picture of the study guide that she'd texted to Lylah on Monday evening. She zoomed in and began copying the answers to the questions she had left blank.

She was nearly finished when she glanced at Lylah, who was looking at her with a disapproving frown. "What are you doing?" she mouthed silently.

Jojo glared and turned to find Mr. Porter looking straight at her. She quickly looked down and covered her phone with her jacket.

Mr. Porter rose to his feet and walked straight to her desk. Very quietly he picked up her test and said, "Come with me."

"Cheating, Jojo? Seriously?" Matt's exasperated voice filled the room. His shoes sounded on the wood floor with every step he took, pacing back and forth.

Jojo sat on the couch, hugging a pillow, watching him go back and forth in front of her. Pastor Jeffreys, the principal of the school, had called Matt to come in when Mr. Porter found her cheating. To his credit, Matt didn't automatically believe them. He had asked her if it was true. She had started to lie, but something stopped her. She couldn't do it. They hadn't suspended her, but she had pleaded with him to just take her home. He hadn't said a single word since they left the school, until now.

Jojo hadn't been able to tell what he was thinking while he was driving home. She had a pretty good idea though. She knew he had to be madder than she had ever seen him, but she wasn't afraid of him. She knew in her heart that he would never hit her like Brent had so many times. Brent never really had a good reason, but Matt did. Still, she knew he wouldn't do it.

That thought should have been comforting, but it wasn't. She squeezed that pillow as hard as she could. Her body was so rigid and tight that she thought she might explode. She held her breath, waiting for him to say the words she knew were coming.

Just say it! Just say you're done. You've had enough of me and all the trouble I've caused. Just say it and let's get the pain over with!

He stopped pacing and stood looking down at her. He took a deep breath then asked, "Why did you do it? You're such a good student. I've seen your grades. Why would you cheat?"

"Please just do it!" Jojo said loudly. "Just say you're sending me back!"

"What? No! What are you talking about?" He sounded alarmed as he sat down beside her on the couch.

"You've had enough of me now, just say it! You're going to send me back!" She hugged the pillow even tighter.

"Is that what you want?" Matt asked. "Is that why you did it? You thought that would be the best way to get out of here?"

"No!" Jojo cried. "I don't want to go, but I know how this works. I mess up bad enough and it's all over."

"No, Jojo," Matt replied calmly. "That's not how we do things in this family. Nobody leaves when things get tough. Families work things out."

"But I'm not really your family," Jojo whispered. "You don't have to keep me."

"You *are* my family. Whether or not my name is on an adoption certificate, you *are* forever a part of my family. Do you understand, Jojo? You're my girl, no matter what you do."

"I'm really your girl?" She couldn't believe he wanted to keep her.

He wrapped his arms around her and kissed the top of her head. She loved when he did that. It made her feel so safe and protected, and her body was learning to stay relaxed. "Jojo, what do you say we call Erica and tell her we want to start the adoption process? You could officially become Jojo Morris."

This could be my forever family!

She looked Matt in the eye and nodded. She did want to be adopted. She did want to be a Morris. A peace settled over her, and she took a deep breath. *Joanna Joy Morris, I like the sound of that.*

He hugged her again. "Amber should be here very soon; I can't wait to tell her!" He leaned back and continued, "We still have this cheating issue to discuss. Why did you do it?"

"I had to," she started. "I know it was my fault that I forgot about the test, but I can't afford a bad grade! I had to find a way to pass that test."

"Why do you think you had to pass that test? It's one test, Jojo. Really, what's one bad grade in the big picture?" Matt asked.

"I *have* to get good grades. I want to get a scholarship to a good college. I want to make something of myself someday."

"Honey, you're not going to miss out on a scholarship because of one low grade."

"You don't understand. School is the one thing that I can control. It's the one thing I'm good at. Besides, copying a few answers on that test wasn't hurting anyone else. I would have known them if I hadn't forgotten about the test being today. What's the big deal anyway?" She pulled the pillow back into a hug.

"The big deal is that it's wrong."

"Why? If I was working in a science laboratory somewhere and I didn't know the answer to something, I'd look it up in a reference book. What's the difference really?"

"That's a valid question. The difference is that when you were taking that test, your intention was to turn it in to Mr. Porter for a grade. You were saying to him that those were your answers. When, in fact, they were not. When you say or do things that make others believe a falsehood, what is that?"

She shrugged.

He waited.

"A lie, I guess."

"The Bible says that lying is a sin. Do you know what a sin is?"

"Not exactly, something bad I guess."

"Yes, a sin is anything we do that goes against God's Word. Have you ever heard of the Ten Commandments?" Matt asked.

"You mean like do not kill and stuff like that?"

"Exactly. God gave those commandments so we can see that we all are sinners. Every person who has ever lived, except one, has broken at least one of those commandments."

"So, there's just ten rules to know?"

Matt laughed a little. "Well, no, but those ten are a good place to start."

"So, who is the one person who never sinned?"

"Jesus. He is God's Son, and He came to earth as a baby to be our Savior."

"Huh?" Jojo asked.

"You see, God is a righteous, holy God. He is only good, and He cannot be where sin is. He tells us in His Word that we are all sinners. We're born that way."

"Babies are sinners? They can't even do anything." Jojo said.

"You're right but think about a baby who is just learning to walk. Does anyone have to teach that baby to disobey its parents? Let's say it's a little boy and he wants a cookie, but it's almost dinner time, so his mom tells him no. Do you think someone had to teach that baby to scream and cry because he wants something he can't have?"

"No, I guess not," she answered, understanding.

"Well, the Bible tells us that we are all born like that. We are all sinners. And it says that the wages, or the penalty, for sin is death and separation from God when we die. But the best news of all is that Jesus loved us so much that he came to earth, the only one who has never sinned, to pay the price for our sins. He died in our place! All we have to do is accept that free gift He offers us."

"Wait, what do you mean accept it? How do you accept it?"

"To accept God's gift of salvation means that we believe it and we receive it for ourselves. It's like your teddy bear. When Eli held out that bag, you had to take it. The gift was for you, but you could have said no, you didn't want it."

Well, if lying is a sin, I proved I'm a sinner today. I know I've done many bad things in my life. Sometimes I get mad at God, but I don't want to be separated from Him forever.

"How do I do it? Accept it, I mean?"

"It's very easy. The Bible says in Romans chapter six that the wages of sin is death, but the gift of God is eternal life through Jesus Christ our Lord. So, do you believe you are a sinner, and that the penalty for sin is death and being separated from God forever in Hell?"

"Yes," Jojo answered sincerely, "I do believe that, and I guess I proved it today in science class."

"And, do you believe that Jesus, God's Son, died to pay that penalty for you?"

"Yes, I believe that too."

"Then the Bible says in Romans chapter ten that whoever calls, or believes, on the name of the Lord, shall be saved. So, you just need to pray and ask the Lord to forgive you of your sins and be your Savior, and He will. Then you will be saved and have eternal life in Heaven!"

"I want to do that!" Jojo said. "Can I do it now?"

"Absolutely!"

And she did.

Amber got home and walked into the room just as Jojo was finishing her prayer. Matt stood up and wiped tears from his eyes. "Tell her all your good news, Jojo!"

"I just got saved!" Jojo exclaimed joyfully, jumping to her feet. "And Matt's going to call Erica and tell her I want you to adopt me!"

"Oh, Jojo!" Amber cried and hugged her close. "This is wonderful news! I'm so excited! What brought all this on? Why are you even home from school already?"

"Let's sit down," Matt said. "We still have some things to discuss. Right, Jojo?"

Her smile faded a little, but not too much because she had so much to be happy about at the moment.

Jojo realized that she'd done the wrong thing by cheating on that test. Pastor Jeffreys had already said she was getting a zero for her grade. Matt took her phone for an undetermined amount of time. He said he needed to think about it a while. But the hardest part was that she had to apologize to Mr. Porter and Pastor Jeffreys tomorrow. "It'll be hard, Jojo. But trust me, you'll be really glad you did it in the end," Matt assured her. "Pray about it. The Lord will help you to have the courage you need and the right words to say."

"We'll be praying for you too, Jojo," Amber added. "You can do this! With God's help you can do anything!"

Matt asked Jojo if she'd like to call Lylah and tell her all of her good news. "You're still grounded from your phone, but I'll make this one exception since it's so important."

"Thank you!" He handed the phone to her and she ran to her room to make the call.

Lylah was just as excited as she was about her adoption and especially about her getting saved. "This is just, it's, well, I don't even know a word for how awesome this is!"

Jojo laughed, "Me either!" They chatted for a few minutes, but Jojo figured she'd better not stay on too long. "I'll see you tomorrow. Oh, and I have to leave early again tomorrow because I have a doctor's appointment. Will you take good notes for me in history class?"

"I'll try," Lylah agreed. "Good-night!"

Dr. Lindsay's office was pretty quiet on Thursday afternoon. The receptionist talked on the telephone and there was a cartoon playing on a television in the corner, but nobody was watching it. In fact, the waiting area was empty except for Amber and Jojo. "Did you have a chance to talk to Mr. Porter or Pastor Jeffreys today? How did it go?"

"Yes, I talked to both of them before school. I couldn't stand to wait any longer. It was so embarrassing, but you were right. I'm glad I did it. They both said they forgive me."

"I'm really proud of you, you know that? That was a very difficult and mature thing to do." Amber moved a curl off of Jojo's forehead. "Your hair is really starting to grow. Do you like it?"

"I like it better than it was after I cut it, but I can't wait for it to get long again."

"Aren't you thankful for second chances?" Amber asked, smiling. "We do something we regret, and those things often have consequences that we don't like, but God forgives us."

"What if we mess up again, after he's already forgiven us once?"

"He will never give up on you, no matter how many times you mess up. God always forgives. He doesn't just give second chances; His grace is unending. It's kind of like your hair. No matter how many times you cut it, it's always going to grow back. Right?"

"Joanna?" a lady's voice interrupted.

"That's us," Amber said. "She prefers to be called Jojo."

The nurse led them to an exam room at the end of a short hallway. She took Jojo's temperature and said, "You have a slight fever, did you know that?"

Jojo shook her head.

"No," Amber answered, "we didn't realize it."

"Okay, Dr. Lindsay will be in very shortly."

As the nurse left the room Amber asked, "Do you feel bad?"

"No," Jojo answered, "not really. I'm tired, but I don't feel bad."

Dr. Lindsay came in and shook Jojo's hand. "I'm Heather Lindsay. It's nice to meet you, Jojo." She wasn't much taller than Jojo and had very curly brown hair and round glasses. "What brings you in today?"

They three spent the next several minutes discussing Jojo's situation. Then Dr. Lindsay did a brief examination, noting Jojo's bruises in particular.

"We need to start by getting some blood work. I'm putting the order in now," she said as she typed into her computer. "I'd like you to go over to the lab at the hospital and get that taken care of today. Once we see those results, we'll know a lot more about what's going on."

"Do you think it could be that she needs a particular vitamin or something like that?" Amber asked.

"That's very possible," Dr. Lindsay answered. "It's just hard to say without seeing those blood test results."

"Okay, well I can take her to get that done right now then."

"Great, the lab is usually pretty quick, so I'll have someone call you with the results and we'll go from there."

"Sounds good," Amber said. "You ready, Jojo?"

"Is this going to hurt?" she asked.

"Just a pinch," Dr. Lindsay answered.

Amber said she expected someone from Dr. Lindsay's office would probably call the next day, so they were both surprised when Amber's cell phone rang while they sat in line at the McDonald's drive thru a short time after leaving the hospital. For some reason Amber picked up her phone and answered it instead of letting the SUV's speakerphone pick up.

"Hello," she said. "Yes, this is Amber … Oh, hi Dr. Lindsay. I didn't expect to hear from you this soon … What ..."

Jojo watched Amber turn her face away, looking out the driver's side window. *What's going on?* Jojo could hear Dr. Lindsay's voice, but couldn't make out what she was saying.

"Okay, I understand …" Amber's voice sounded shaky. "It's almost five now? We can be there by six thirty… Okay… Okay… Bye."

"What?" Jojo asked, feeling suddenly very scared. Her hands began shaking.

Amber reached over and put her hand over Jojo's. "Dr. Lindsay says we need to get you to the hospital in Morgantown right away."

"Why?" Jojo could feel the tears pooling in her eyes.

"I need to get out of this line," Amber said looking behind them.

"Why?" Jojo asked again.

Amber pulled the vehicle into a parking spot and turned to face Jojo. She took Jojo's hand in hers and said, "Dr. Lindsay says that your white blood cell count is extremely high, and they need to run more tests right away."

"Tests for what?"

"They think that you maybe have a cancer called leukemia."

Jojo's heart felt as if it stopped beating. Her body stiffened. *I what? That can't be right! God wouldn't let that happen, would He? Not when I am just starting to enjoy my new family! Does this mean they won't want to adopt me, a sick kid?*

CHAPTER 9

The next several minutes were a blur to Jojo. They drove home, packed an overnight bag for Jojo, and Matt drove them to the hospital, which was an hour away. Amber sat in the backseat with Jojo, holding her hand for the entire trip. Matt pulled into the parking garage but stopped them from getting out right away. "Let's pray before we go in."

He turned sideways in his seat and held Jojo's hand, while Amber wrapped her arms tightly around her. He thanked God for Jojo and asked Him to protect her and take care of her. He continued, "Lord, if it's Your will, please let there be no cancer in Jojo's body. But, God, if that's not Your will. please help us to accept what comes. Walk through this valley with us. Give Jojo peace. Help her not to be afraid."

When he finished praying, they walked in with Matt holding one of her hands, and Amber holding the other. They checked in and were immediately taken to a room in the WVU Children's Hospital. The room had blue walls with pictures of superheroes painted on them. There was a large window overlooking the parking lot below. Beyond that, Jojo could see a huge football stadium. As Amber helped Jojo get settled on the bed, Matt explained that stadium was where the WVU Mountaineers played. He set Jojo's bag on a little brown couch that was situated under the window, and Amber sat down in a reclining chair that was sitting between the couch and the hospital bed. Jojo noticed there were a couple other chairs sitting along the opposite wall, and there was a door leading to the bathroom in the corner by the window.

A bubbly nurse named Emily was the first to enter Jojo's room. "Hi, Jojo! I'm Emily! I get to be your nurse tonight. We'll get you all settled in and comfortable in no time." She checked the wristband they had put on Jojo when she first entered the hospital. "What's your birthday?"

"October tenth."

"Perfect, that's exactly what your bracelet says. One thing about it here, we do ask a lot of questions."

Jojo felt weird lying in a hospital bed with her clothes on.

"Did you have dinner yet?" Emily asked.

"No, but I'm not really hungry."

"How about something little? Maybe a grilled cheese sandwich?"

"I don't know." Jojo's stomach was churning; she didn't know if she could keep anything down if she tried to eat.

"Well, I'll order you one, just in case." Emily said with a smile. "Now, my friend Stephen is coming in a few minutes to draw some blood. You've already done that once today, right?" Jojo nodded. "So, you know this won't be so bad. Then we'll leave you alone for a little while so you can get settled in. Mom and Dad," she said to Amber and Matt, "do you need anything right now?"

Matt looked at Amber and started to say something then stopped. Then he answered, "I think we're fine for right now."

"Alright, I need to get an IV started in you, Jojo. Don't worry though, I'm very good at this. I've done more of these than I could begin to count." She set a tray on the table beside her and began to place the IV in Jojo's left arm.

Matt's cell phone rang. He looked at the screen and said, "It's Erica, I'll be right back."

He left the room and Jojo frowned.

Emily finished the IV and said, "That's it. Stephen will be in shortly. Just push this button right here if you need me," she said pointing to a button on a remote that was connected to her bed. "Oh, you can also control your TV with these buttons. And these," she said pointing again, "will adjust your bed when you want to sit up or lay back." Then she left the room.

"What was that frown for?" Amber asked, scooting her chair closer to the bed.

"I hate when people talk about me behind my back, that's all." She lay her head on the pillow and closed her eyes.

"They're not talking behind your back, Jojo. Matt just didn't want to try to have a conversation on his phone while Emily was trying to talk to you, that's all."

"Why is he even talking to Erica anyway?"

"She's your social worker, so we have to keep her updated about how you're doing and what's happening."

"Okay."

What's going to happen to me? Am I dying? God, I'm so scared. Tears started stinging her eyes, but Jojo took a deep breath and blinked them away. She was worried that if she started crying, she wouldn't be able to stop.

Amber ran her fingers through Jojo's hair and quietly whispered, "I love you, Jojo."

Stephen came in and explained that he was a phlebotomist. When Jojo asked what that meant, he replied, "It means I have the best job in the hospital. I get to push my cart around and take people's blood all day." He paused and put a pair of fake teeth with long fangs in his mouth. "I'm like a real-life vampire. But don't tell anyone. I try to keep my fangs hidden."

Matt returned just as Stephen was pushing his phlebotomy cart back into the hallway. "Did that guy have fangs?" he asked looking back over his shoulder.

"He sure did," Amber said.

"He's weird," Jojo added.

The next couple of hours were fairly quiet. Jojo's dinner tray came, but she didn't eat much. Matt and Amber hadn't had dinner either, but Matt said he would go get them something after the doctor came in. He didn't want to miss hearing what he had to say.

Dr. O'Malley finally came in a few minutes before nine. He pulled a rolling stool from underneath the counter beside the door and over to the side of Jojo's bed. Right away Jojo thought he had kind eyes and she liked the way he spoke directly to her.

"Hi, Jojo, I'm Dr. O'Malley." He smiled and held out his hand for her to shake.

"Hi," she said, shaking his hand.

"I'm a pediatric oncologist, which means I am a doctor who specializes in treating cancer in young people like you. Unfortunately, Jojo, I'm afraid I have some bad news. But I also have some good news. If it's okay with you, I'm going to start with the bad news and get that out of the way. Sound good?"

She nodded.

"The bad news is we believe you have a cancer called leukemia," Dr. O'Malley explained. Matt, who was standing at the head of Jojo's bed, reached for her hand and held it tight. "We believe this because we can see an abnormally high amount of white blood cells in your blood, and we see lower than normal red blood cells and platelets. We also see some cells called blasts. These are actually white blood cells that haven't fully developed. This is the reason you've had so many bruises lately. So, the next thing we need to do is determine exactly what type of leukemia you have. Then we will be able to make a plan for your treatment. Does that make sense?"

She nodded again.

"Now, in order to determine what type we're dealing with, we need to do a bone marrow aspiration and a bone marrow biopsy. These are two tests that we will actually do at the same time. What happens is we use a needle to take some bone marrow, that's the stuff found inside your bones, and a small piece of bone from the large hip bone in you lower back."

"Will that hurt?" Jojo asked, feeling panicked.

"Don't worry," Dr. O'Malley said calmly. "We'll give you medicine to make you comfortable. You will basically sleep through the entire thing."

"When will you do this?" Matt asked.

"Since she's already had some food this evening, we'll wait until morning. It will likely be fairly early. I'd guess around five or five-thirty. We'll let you know."

Jojo squeezed Matt's hand tightly. *I'm so scared.*

"Now," Dr. O'Malley continued, "do you have any questions before we go on, Jojo?"

She shook her head. Her mind was spinning, and she couldn't seem to think straight.

"Very well. You stop me, if you think of anything, okay?"

She nodded.

"Once we get the results of those tests, we'll know more of what we're dealing with. Now we come to the good news. Are you ready for some good news, Jojo?"

She nodded again.

"The good news is, you are in the best hospital in the state, and we are going to do everything we can to make sure you have a full recovery."

"So, does that mean there's a chance I might die?" Jojo could feel her heart beating rapidly. Amber stood and took Jojo's other hand in hers.

"Jojo, I don't believe in lying to my patients. So, believe me when I say that while that is a slight possibility, I believe it is very unlikely. And, I give you my word that I will do everything within my power to make sure that you live a long and happy life."

Matt used a tissue to wipe the tears from Jojo's eyes.

"Try to get some rest tonight, Jojo. I'll be back to see you tomorrow, probably before lunchtime. We'll know a lot more by then and we'll get this sorted out. Good-night, dear."

Once the doctor left, Jojo began to cry again. This time Matt and Amber shed some tears with her. After a few minutes, Matt prayed for her again. He leaned over the top of her bed to turn out the light. "Please don't leave me alone," Jojo pleaded.

"Don't you worry, kiddo. I'm not going anywhere." He kissed the top of her head and sat down in the reclining chair beside her bed. Amber was sitting in another chair beside Jojo's bed.

"Jojo, we won't ever leave you alone. I promise that at least one of us will always be with you, okay?" Amber said.

"Thanks," Jojo whispered.

"Want me to lie with you until you fall asleep?" Amber asked.

Jojo nodded and scooted over to make room. Amber carefully settled in the bed beside Jojo, holding her close.

"One of my favorite Bible verses is Psalm fifty-six, verse three. It says, 'What time I am afraid, I will trust in Thee.' I know you're afraid right now, Jojo. I am too. But God is always good. We can trust Him. This might be a long, hard road, but you'll never walk it alone."

"I'm so glad you're here," Jojo whispered.

"Me too. You know, this was a big surprise to us, but God knew this was coming. He made sure you had a family to love you through this. And that's exactly what we're going to do."

Thank you for giving me a family, God.

"Try to get some sleep, okay?" Amber whispered. "We're not going anywhere. You're safe."

It took a long time, but Jojo finally drifted to sleep. It didn't last very long though, because a man named Chris came to take her for the bone marrow aspiration and biopsy at five o'clock the next morning.

"I'm going to run home and get the dogs taken care of. Amber, I'll get the things you wanted. Jojo, is there anything you want me to bring from home?" Matt asked.

"My schoolbooks and Chromebook." Suddenly a new fear popped into her head. "How am I going to keep up with school?" *I can't get behind!*

"I'll bring what you have at home, and I'll call the school. We'll make sure we get everything worked out. Don't worry."

"I don't want to fail!"

"You won't. I promise I'll get it all taken care of today. Okay?" Matt reassured.

"Okay," she agreed. What else could she say?

"We'd better get going," Chris said.

"Okay," Matt said. "Amber will stay with you, and I'll be back before the doctor comes in. I'll see ya shortly. I love you."

Jojo smiled at him and said, "Bye."

Jojo was brought back to her room about an hour later. The numbing medicine was starting to wear off and she was starting to feel some pain. The nurse gave her medicine for it. She watched a bit of TV and dozed on and off. Matt came in around ten o'clock and Dr. O'Malley came in a little before eleven. Jojo was so nervous to hear what he had to say. *Hurry up! Just tell me what's going to happen!*

The doctor rolled a stool over again and sat beside Jojo. "Good morning. Did you get any sleep last night?"

She shrugged.

"She slept a little," Amber answered for her.

"I got your test results back this morning and discussed the results with the team. Now, I'm going to give you a lot of information right now. You may not remember it all, and that's okay. If you don't understand something, or you have a question, please stop me and ask. Okay?"

Jojo nodded.

"You have what's called acute myeloid leukemia. We want to get rid of this cancer as soon as possible, so we're going to get started today. Your treatment will be in two phases. The first phase is induction. It is a combination of chemotherapy and medications that will stop abnormal cells from being made in your bone marrow. The goal of this phase is to get the cancer to go into remission. This means leukemia cells are no longer visible under the microscope when we look at either your bone marrow or blood.

"The induction phase will probably last approximately four weeks. Then we'll give you a break for a week or so, then do it again."

"Will I have to stay in the hospital the whole time?" Jojo asked.

"Yes. This is a pretty aggressive type of cancer, so we are going to treat it aggressively. The chemo will probably have some unpleasant side effects. You may have nausea, but we can give you medicine to help that. You'll probably lose your hair. It's a little hard to say because everyone's body reacts differently to chemotherapy.

"We'll put a port in your chest so you won't have to keep the IV the whole time. We will put the chemo medicine right in your port. Then ten days later we'll do it again, then again in another ten days. Then we'll give you a break. We'll do another bone marrow biopsy to make sure the chemo is doing its job. You might get to go home that week; we'll have to see.

"Then we'll bring you back for a second round of three treatments. After that, if everything goes like we hope and there are no signs of the leukemia, you'll be ready for phase two, which is consolidation. We'll do that to kill any lingering cells that may be hiding in there somewhere.

"That was a lot. Do you have any questions?"

"You said if everything goes like we hope, what if it doesn't?"

"Good question," Dr. O'Malley answered. "Two cycles of chemo may not be enough. If it's not, we'll do it again."

"Are there any clinical trials that she should be part of?" Matt asked.

"What's that?" Jojo asked, looking at Matt.

Dr. O'Malley answered, "A clinical trial means using new treatments that we are currently developing here. I was just talking to my collogues about that earlier. I believe this combination we're starting today will be quite effective. However, we are seeing some very promising results from a few trials right now. So, we will definitely be looking into that for her as well. I'll keep you updated about that."

Jojo tried to process all the information she just heard. Suddenly she remembered what he'd said about her hair. *I'll lose my hair?* Her stomach dropped.

Amber must have noticed the funny look on her face. "What is it, Jojo? You suddenly look troubled."

"I'm going to lose my hair. Like, all of it?" She couldn't believe it.

"You will more than likely lose some hair, maybe even all of it," Dr. O'Malley said with a sympathetic smile.

"But it will grow back, sweetheart," Amber said. "Remember? Hair always grows back!"

"But I'm going to be bald?" She wiped at the fresh tears.

"Hey, you'll look like me for a few weeks," Matt said with a grin.

"That is probably not a big comfort, Matt," Amber said.

"I know this is difficult to hear, but we really do have to just wait and see," Dr. O'Malley explained.

After a few more questions, Dr. O'Malley left, and very shortly her nurse for the day, Julie, brought in the chemotherapy and began her first treatment. The rest of the day was pretty quiet. Jojo ate lunch but didn't feel like eating much dinner. Jojo's head was spinning with thoughts of cancer and treatments and side effects. It was all very overwhelming, so she tried to make herself stop thinking about it. Matt suggested they watch a movie, so she tried to focus on that. They were all pretty exhausted and fell asleep early.

Sometime early the next morning Jojo woke up feeling very nauseas and started throwing up. Emily, her night nurse, came in to help care for her.

"I'll call Dr. O'Malley and tell him we need to increase your nausea medication. That will help you feel better," she said.

A while later the nausea had eased, probably due to the medicine Emily had given her, and Jojo fell asleep again. Emily had told her the increased medicine would probably make her sleepy, and it did. She slept for much of the day. Finally, around dinnertime, she felt more awake.

She looked over to the little couch that turned into a bed where Matt and Amber were discussing whether or not he should go home for the night and go to church tomorrow. "This is going to be a long process," Amber commented. "You need to go home and work."

Matt glanced over to the bed. "Hey, sleepy-head, you're awake! How are you feeling?"

"Better, I think," Jojo answered. Her voice sounded scratchy. She tried to sit up.

"Wait," Amber said coming over to her bed. "Use this remote to make your bed sit up. You want to sit up slowly, so you don't get sick again."

"Are you leaving?" Jojo asked Matt. *Please don't leave me here with this terrified feeling!* Only a little while ago, she didn't want to be with Matt, but now the thought of him walking out the door was worse than the memory of losing Lamby.

Matt walked over to her bed and sat on the edge. "We were just discussing that. How do you feel about me going home tonight? Amber would stay here with you, of course, and I'll come back Monday morning."

He has things he needs to do. He'll come back though. "It's fine, you need to go home for church," Jojo answered.

"Are you sure that's okay with you? I can get someone to preach for me if I need to."

"I'm sure. There's nothing you can do here."

"Is it okay if I tell the people at church what's going on? They love you, and they'll be praying for you."

More people talking about me? But talking about me to God is maybe a different kind of talking. "I guess so," Jojo said, thinking maybe more prayers would be good.

"Do you want to call Lylah yourself tonight and tell her, or would you rather I just tell her?"

"You do it. I don't think I want to talk about it." Jojo looked down and started picking at a fingernail.

"You don't have to talk about it if you don't want to," Matt said. "I need to call Eli too."

"Erica stopped by today while you were sleeping," Amber said.

Jojo's head jerked up, "Why? What did she want? Are they going to make me go to a different hospital or something?" *Why do they have to control my life so much? It's not fair.*

"No, nothing like that," Matt reassured. "Her job is to help take care of you, Jojo. She really does care about you."

"She's always taking me from one house to another. Why can't she just leave me alone? She's nosy; always talking behind my back to my teachers and you and whoever else she feels like," Jojo argued.

"I'm sorry it feels that way. She did give us some good news though," Matt said.

Jojo looked up at him but didn't respond.

"I asked her if this would mean that the adoption process couldn't begin, but she said this shouldn't change any of that. She's already started working on the paperwork."

Some of Jojo's scared-ness relaxed a little. *I thought Matt and Amber might change their minds; why would they want to adopt a sick girl? But I guess they still want me.* "Good," Jojo said.

"I agree!" Amber added enthusiastically.

"Me too!" Matt added. "I guess I'd better get going soon. Did you think of anything you want from home?"

"Would you bring my gray jacket?" Amber asked. "It gets chilly in here sometimes."

"Jojo?"

She wanted to ask him to bring her new teddy bear, but felt silly about it, so she said, "Nothing, I guess."

"Call if you think of anything." He stood and kissed Amber goodbye. Then he kissed Jojo on the head and said, "Bye, kiddo. I love you."

"Bye," she whispered.

Later, after Amber had turned off the lights and they were both settled in for the night, Jojo allowed herself to really think about what was happening to her. *I have cancer. I. Have. Cancer. Dr. O'Malley said we have to wait to see what will happen. "Don't worry" he said. How am I supposed to not worry? Will I lose my hair? If I do, I'm going to be so ugly! What about school? Dr. O'Malley said I have to stay here for at least four weeks, then maybe go home for one, and come back here for another four weeks! I am going to miss the whole end of the year! God, I'm trying to trust you like Amber said, but I cannot afford to fail seventh grade! I don't want to be ugly. And, God, what if this treatment doesn't work?*

CHAPTER 10

Jojo felt pretty sick for the first couple of days after her initial chemo treatment, but by the sixth day, she was feeling better and getting bored. She did get tired easily though and took a lot of naps. Her nurses and other hospital caregivers were very friendly and did a good job of trying to keep her mind occupied. There were video game systems available, a playroom with toys for smaller children, and a basketball game similar to what you'd find at a county fair.

Matt, surprising her again by somehow knowing what she wanted without her saying so, had brought her teddy bear and phone to her, so she texted Lylah now and then. He and Amber played board games with her, watched movies, and helped her with her schoolwork whenever she felt up to doing it. Pastor Jeffreys had been in the day before for a quick visit. He told Jojo that he had made arrangements with all of the teachers for her to finish out the year online. He said they were very willing to extend any deadlines, even into the summer. "We know how important school is to you," he had said. "It's important to us too. But don't worry about trying to do schoolwork on the days you're feeling sick. We'll help you get through this."

That was a huge relief to Jojo. Still, she had tried to work extra hard these last couple of days to make up for the days she'd already missed.

Eli called her one evening and joked around with her for a while. "You're officially going to be my little sister pretty soon, and I am finished with school in another week, so you'd better watch out. I'll be there to pick on you before you know it!"

"You wouldn't pick on a sick kid, would you?" Jojo teased back.

"You never know. Dad said there's a basketball game there, and that you're a pretty good shot."

"I beat him today!" Jojo announced proudly.

"Good for you! Well, I need to go. I'll talk to you soon, okay?"

"Okay, bye."

"I'm praying for you, little sister. Bye."

The day after her second round of chemo was a little better than after the first round because they gave her a larger dose of nausea medicine to begin with. But the day after that was her worst day yet. She went into the bathroom and looked at herself in the mirror. Her scalp was hurting a little and she ran her fingers gently through her hair. She ended up with two handfuls of it. She sucked in a breath and held it. Even though she knew losing her hair was a possibility, she was shocked to find her hands full of her own hair. Instantly her eyes starting stinging with tears. "Amber," she called.

Amber opened the door and rushed in. Her eyes went first to Jojo's face, then to her hands full of hair. "Oh, sweetheart," she whispered. "It's going to be okay." She pulled the trashcan out from under the sink with her foot and helped Jojo put the hair in it. "Come here," she said and wrapped her in a hug.

After a moment, Jojo got her tears under control and they went back into her room. Amber pulled one of the chairs into the middle of the floor and had Jojo sit on it. "My head is sore," Jojo told her.

Amber used a brush and gently brushed out all the loose hair. Even though Jojo's hair was still short, and only part of it had fallen out so far, there was quite a pile of hair after she finished. Emily was her nurse again this day, and she walked in as Amber was finishing up the brushing. "Have you thought about what you want to do about your hair?" she asked.

"What do you mean?" Jojo asked.

"A lot of people say their head is sore, and they don't like their hair falling out everywhere, so they decide to cut their hair super short, or even just shave it off."

Shave my head? Jojo was shocked she would even suggest such a thing.

Emily continued, "If you don't want to go that route, I can bring you a little cap to wear for a few days until it all comes out."

My hair is all going to fall out! I'm going to be bald and ugly! Just like that kid I saw in the playroom yesterday who had no hair; even his eyebrows and eyelashes were gone. I'm going to look like that.

Jojo looked at Emily but couldn't make her mouth say any words. Finally, Amber suggested they try a cap, at least for now. Emily brought one in and Amber put it carefully on Jojo's sore head.

Amber helped Jojo get back in bed and said, "You know, I bet your head would quit hurting if we just shaved the hair off."

Jojo figured she was probably right, but she couldn't imagine herself bald.

"I know this is not what you wanted but try to remember that this medicine is saving your life. And, this hair loss is only temporary. Remember, hair always grows back!"

"Matt's doesn't," Jojo pointed out.

"Okay," Amber agreed, giggling a little, "but his case is different. He has a bald spot because of genetics, so he shaves off the rest to even it out. That's not what's going to happen with you. Your hair is falling out because of a medicine, but as soon as the medicine is out of your body, your hair will grow back. And, most of Matt's hair grows back too, he just doesn't like the way it looks."

God, why are you doing this to me? "Well, what if I say I'm really mad at God for allowing me to get cancer? And I'm really mad at him for letting my hair fall out?"

"He's a big God, Jojo, and he can handle it. You might as well say it anyway, because he already knows it. But don't stay mad too long. It really only hurts you. I have no idea why God allows things like this. We will probably never really know the answer to that question. But the thing I do know is that he loves you enough to give his life for you. He created you, and he wants to help you through this if you'll let him."

I'm still mad.

Matt came in later that evening and offered to shave Jojo's head for her. She was surprised at herself, but she agreed to let him do it. Her head was sore, and she had found a bunch of hair in her plate at lunch. *If it's all going to come out anyway, I might as well get it over with.*

It only took a few minutes to do it, and her head did feel better with the hair gone. Jojo stared at herself in the mirror afterwards, trying to get used to seeing herself this way. Amber went down to the gift shop and returned with a purple scarf and a multicolored soft hat for Jojo to try. *This is definitely going to take some time to get used to. I look like an ugly alien.*

She managed to hold in her tears until they went to bed. Then she cried silently into her pillow until she fell asleep.

Jojo was staring at her reflection in the bathroom mirror after brushing her teeth two days later when Amber called, "Jojo! Come see who's here!"

She put the multicolored hat on her bald head and opened the bathroom door to find Lylah and her mom sitting on the little couch waiting for her. Lylah jumped up and hugged Jojo tight. Jojo wanted to go back into the bathroom to hide. *They must think I look so ugly and pathetic.*

"You didn't tell me about your hair yet," Lylah said, getting right to the point faster than anyone else Jojo had ever known.

"It just happened a couple days ago," Jojo said, trying to pull the hat lower on her head.

"I'm sorry it had to happen, but I love your hat! It's really cute!" Lylah's sweet words made Jojo's racing heart slow down a bit.

"How are you feeling today?" Michelle asked.

"I feel good today. I just get tired easy, that's all."

"We brought you a gift from Miss Evie," Michelle said. "She and Mr. John have had colds, so they didn't want to risk coming to visit right now, but she sent some treats for you. She said she knows you love cookies."

"I do love her cookies," Jojo said with a smile. "I don't usually feel like eating very much though."

Amber explained, "She had about two good days after her first treatment where we could get her to eat something more than a few bites. I think her appetite is coming back again today. She ate all of her breakfast for the first time since we've been here."

"Oh, Jojo, you have to see how the baby goats have grown," Lylah said pulling out her phone. The girls settled on Jojo's bed to chat while Amber and Michelle were sitting on the couch doing the same thing.

All of a sudden, Amber said, "Jojo, here he comes!"

Jojo immediately fell back on her pillow, pulled her fluffy purple blanket over her head, and said, "Don't let him see me!"

Amber quickly moved the other bed sheets and blankets up, so it looked more like a pile of bed clothes than a person.

"Hey, Brandon," Amber said to the nurse as he entered the room pushing a computer cart.

"Hey, Miss Amber, how are you ladies on this fine day?"

"We're great. These are our friends, Michelle and Lylah."

"Nice to meet you. I see we're missing the star of the show. Where is she?"

Jojo popped up and yelled, "Gotcha!"

Startled, Brandon laughed and said, "Ha, you did."

The ladies all giggled, and Brandon said, "I guess you owed me that."

Jojo explained, "He squirted me with a water gun this morning! Can you believe that?" She pretended to be offended.

"You just about scared me to death!" Brandon argued. "You'd better watch out. I have a long memory."

They all laughed again, and Jojo thought how great it felt to laugh again. Even Matt, who was usually always joking around, had been very serious lately.

Brandon checked Jojo's temperature and gave her some medication, then left.

"Can I take Lylah down to the playroom for a little while?" Jojo asked Amber.

"Sure, we'll come find you in a little while."

"The nurses call it the playroom because it has toys for little kids, but it's really a big open area with tables to play games or work puzzles on, a large screen TV, computers, game systems, bean bags, and all sorts of other things." As they headed out the door, Jojo added, "Surprisingly, it's not usually crowded at all. I guess sick kids don't feel like playing very much."

The girls walked down the hall to the colorful children's play area. They found an open table in the corner and sat on the tall stools, looking out the window. "Have you ever been inside that stadium?" Jojo asked.

"No, I don't really like football. My dad and Uncle John go to games once in a while."

"I don't like football either. I do like baseball though. I'm a pretty good pitcher usually."

"I like to play too. Maybe when you get out of here, we can have another cookout and get some people from our class to come. We could play a game in our big pasture."

"That would be fun. Speaking of school, how's it going?"

"It's school. Everybody misses you though. Ryan said we need to learn to play the video game they play, then we could all play online as a big group."

"What is it called?"

"I don't remember. I'm usually outside." Lylah laughed. "I don't play many video games. But maybe we can learn. It might be fun. I'll find out what it is and text it to you."

"Okay, thanks. How's math going? I know you were worried before."

"Oh, I stink at math! I don't know what I'm going to do. We're supposed to be reviewing the metric system right now. I never did learn it in the first place. I can never remember what's the difference between centi-, milli-, kilo-, and whatever the rest of them are. I'll never be able to figure out how to convert things if I can't even remember what they are!"

"You can do it! It's easy. Let me show you." Jojo hopped off her stool and walked over to the whiteboard that practically filled up one whole wall. "I use the sentence King Henry died under dried cow manure."

"What?" Lylah said walking over to the board and laughing. "I have no idea what you're talking about."

"The first letter of each word of the sentence stands for one of the metric prefixes. See?" Jojo wrote the letters K H D U D C M on the white board. "K, king, stands for kilo-, H, Henry, stands for hecto-, and so on."

"Wait, what's the sentence again?" Lylah asked.

"King Henry died under dried cow manure," Jojo repeated giggling.

Twenty minutes later Lylah not only had the metric prefixes and their values memorized, but she was also converting them. "Jojo, I don't know how you did it. Thank you! You are the best math teacher I ever had!"

Jojo laughed. "It's not as hard as you think. I'm happy to help you. Actually, it's not very often that I get to do something to help someone else."

Lylah said, "Well, get used to helping, because you're going to be my math tutor from now on!" Jojo smiled, liking that idea very much. It wasn't that she was happy Lylah was struggling, but it felt good to be needed for once. *Usually people just want me to stay out of their way. That seems to be changing. Maybe that's the silver lining in all this cancer stuff.*

Later that afternoon Eli finally made it home from college and came to see her. He not only came to visit, but he brought her a special treat. He and Matt had stopped at Rowdy's and got lunch. They ordered her an orange cream milkshake and packed it carefully in a cooler full of ice so that it would still be a milkshake after the hour drive to the hospital.

Jojo was so excited! She actually ate over half of her cheeseburger and finished nearly all of her milkshake. She wanted to go play basketball with Eli, but after her earlier visit with Lylah, she was really tired. She struggled to keep her eyes open.

Amber noticed and said, "Jojo, why don't you snuggle up there and take a little nap?" She handed Jojo her bear and said, "While you sleep, I may go upstairs with Matt to visit Mrs. Martin. She's Miss Evie's sister, and she's here having surgery tomorrow. Is it okay if Eli stays with you? We'll just be upstairs."

"Okay," Jojo said, already almost asleep.

"We'll be back in a short while then," Matt said. "Eli, take good care of our girl."

"I'm on it, Dad."

About an hour later, Jojo awoke and found her whole family sitting in her room, chatting very quietly. "Look who's finally awake," Eli announced.

"How are you feeling, kiddo?" Matt asked.

"I don't know." She giggled, rubbing her eyes. "Fine, I guess."

"What sounds good for dinner?"

Jojo shrugged.

"If you could have anything in the world to eat right now, what would you pick?"

"Orange gumdrops," she answered with a smile.

"You're going to turn into an orange gumdrop if you keep eating so many of those crazy things." He walked over to her bed and asked, "What do you want for dinner? If you eat something that resembles real food, I'll find you some gumdrops."

"I'll try to eat something. I don't know what. Surprise me." She was too tired to make a decision about it.

"Well, Eli and I will go find something. We'll be back in a little while."

"Why don't you take Mom with you?" Eli suggested. "Let her get some fresh air. I'll keep Jojo company for a while."

"Yea, go ahead," Jojo said to Amber. "Eli can stay with me."

"Are you really sure?" Amber said, sounding a bit worried.

"I'm sure. You promised you would always make sure one of you was with me. Well, Eli's with me," Jojo answered.

Amber looked at Matt, then finally agreed to go. "We won't be too long. You have your phone there. Call us if you need anything."

Once they left, Eli pulled his chair closer to her bed. "So, how are you doing? Really?"

"I'm good, I think. The chemo is rough, and makes me sick, but I know it could be worse. I miss my hair." Jojo was thankful that Eli was so easy to talk to. She always felt weird talking to boys, especially ones who were older than her. But talking to Eli was different for some reason. In some ways, it felt like she'd known him her whole life. He treated her just like she imagined any brother treated his little sister.

"At least you can get ready faster in the mornings, right? You don't have to worry about fixing hair you don't have."

"I guess," Jojo conceded. "But I feel like I look so weird and ugly."

"So, what are you going to do about it?" he asked.

"What do you mean? What can I do about it?"

"You can't control a lot of the things that happen to you. But you can control how you respond to those things. You are the one who gets to decide how you feel about things, and how you react to things."

Jojo thought about that. Was that true? *I suppose it is. I get to decide how I feel about things. I get to choose how I react to things. Hummm.*

"You said you feel weird and ugly. You're neither of those things, by the way. But if you feel that way, what are you going to do about it?"

That's a great question. What am I going to do about it?

CHAPTER 11

Jojo was still thinking about what Eli had said while she dressed the next morning. She was looking forward to a day of feeling semi-normal. Though she was still achy and tired, her appetite was better, and the nausea hadn't been too bad. Part of her was glad for the reprieve, but part of her wished she could just get this next cycle over with. She wanted to know if the chemo was really working.

Her head in the mirror's reflection was bald. Her eyebrows and eyelashes were gone too. *I am thankful that there is a chemo they can give me to kill this cancer, but I look so weird. How can I decide to not look weird?* She looked closely at her green eyes. They seemed so bright. *Maybe it's the fluorescent light in this bathroom.* She tied the purple scarf on her head and noticed the way her eyes seemed to look different somehow. She took the scarf off and put on the multicolored hat and examined the difference. A new idea popped into her mind. *Amber said I could pick out some new hats, or scarves, or whatever I want to keep my head comfortable. Maybe I can find something that makes the green in my eyes look brighter.*

She went back into her hospital room and sat on the couch beside Amber. "Do they have any green hats in the gift shop downstairs?" she asked.

"I don't remember seeing any, but we can check. Do you want to try a different style of hat?"

"Maybe," Jojo answered. "I was thinking that maybe a green one would make my eyes look brighter. I feel like I look pale and sick."

Amber smiled and said, "I think that's a great idea. Where's your Chromebook? We can look online and order some if you want. We can always return things you don't like."

"Are you sure?" Jojo asked, thinking that might be a big hassle.

"Of course, I'm sure! Let's look."

Jojo grabbed her computer and they searched through all sorts of shapes, styles, and colors of hats and scarves. She finally decided on a few she'd like to try, and Amber ordered them.

"Now I just need some eyebrows and eyelashes," Jojo commented. "Maybe I should look for some YouTube tutorials on how to draw on eyebrows."

"You can certainly do that," Amber agreed. "I have an eyebrow pencil in my bag in the bathroom if you want to try it. It may not be exactly the right color, but I bet it's close."

Jojo was certainly glad nobody could see some of her first attempts. She and Amber spent most of the morning trying different shapes and techniques, and laughing at all the not-so-perfect eyebrows. It felt good to laugh. And it felt good to regain some control over her appearance. By lunchtime she felt like a new girl. She took some selfies and sent them to Lylah, forgetting that she would still be at school. In moments, Lylah texted back how much everyone liked her new look.

"Oh no!" *She showed my pictures to everyone?* "Who's everyone?" Jojo said aloud as she texted.

Me, Annabeth, Ryan, Aaron, Lindsay, and Miss Collins. It's study hall, and she said we could talk today since it's Friday.

I can't believe you showed my picture to everyone! Lol!

What? You look like your usual beautiful self. I love your eyebrows! High School graduation is tonight. They are posting all their senior pics everywhere, and you look as gorgeous as any of them! Lylah replied. And guess what!!! I got an A on my math test thanks to you! Thank you so much! My dad about had a heart attack. Bell rang, gotta go.

You're welcome, Jojo responded. *Do they really think I look pretty, or are they just being nice? God, I don't understand why this is all happening, but I'm trying to do what everyone keeps telling me. I'm trying to trust you to get me through this. Thanks for giving me sweet friends who try to make me feel better.*

A few days later, Jojo got the news that her counts were too low. Dr. O'Malley explained that the absolute neutrophil count is an estimate of the body's ability to fight infections. Because Jojo's counts were considered very low, she was at a high risk of developing an infection.

"This is quite normal under the circumstances," Dr. O'Malley explained. "In order to try to keep you from developing a dangerous infection, we will be monitoring your temperature very closely. This room you are staying in is set up for isolation, so we won't need to move you. That's why your room opens to that little room with the sink and cabinets instead of the open hallway. You'll need to stay here in your room unless we have to take you for tests somewhere else in the hospital. We'll put a sign on your door requiring all visitors to wash their hands before they come in." He looked at Matt and said, "It's a good idea to limit the people who visit to just immediate family as much as possible."

Jojo glanced up at the bulletin board by the door. It was filled with cards and notes from classmates and people from church. Nearly every day she had a visit from someone. They rarely stayed very long, but she had never had so many people care about her before. She hadn't realized how much she looked forward to and enjoyed those visits. Now, they would have to stop.

"That won't be a problem," Matt assured him.

Dr. O'Malley turned back to Jojo. "No eating fresh fruit or veggies for a while, and no live flowers in your room because they can carry bacteria."

"Is this really bad?" Jojo asked, feeling scared all of a sudden.

"Not necessarily," Dr. O'Malley answered. "It just means that we want to be very careful, so it doesn't turn into something bad. The chemo is doing its job of killing the leukemia cells in your body, but it also affects the good cells. This means that your body doesn't have the ability to fight infections like it normally would."

"How long will this last?" Matt asked.

"It's hard to say," Dr. O'Malley answered. "Today is Tuesday, and she's due for her third treatment on Thursday. We're starting her on a medication to boost her white blood cells today. Hopefully we won't need to delay her chemo. As long as the counts don't go any lower, we'll continue on Thursday."

"When will you do the bone marrow tests to see if the chemo is really working?" Jojo asked.

"We'll give this third round time to work then we'll schedule it." He smiled and said, "Hang in there, Jojo. You're handling all this very well."

Jojo was so tired. She was tired of lying in this bed. She was tired of being poked and examined. She was tired of feeling achy. She was just plain tired. Amber had gone home for a friend's baby shower, so Matt was spending the night with Jojo. He was sitting on the couch, watching a boring movie that she had picked. She had lost interest after the first five minutes. *I can't stand to lie in this bed for one more minute.* She got up, grabbed her bear, and went to sit beside Matt.

"Getting restless?" he asked.

"Yes! I'm so sick of that bed, but I'm too tired to do anything, and my head hurts." She sighed deeply.

"I'm sorry." Matt smiled and put his arm around her.

She leaned her head on his shoulder. *Hugs are nice.*

"Oh," Matt said pulling out his phone. "I forgot to show you this earlier. I thought you might want to see how big the puppies are getting."

He handed her his phone and she scrolled through several adorable puppy pictures. She stopped on a picture of Boone. He was lying on the floor in Jojo's bedroom chewing on a toy. Matt looked at the picture and smiled. "That boy loves two things: sunshine and chewing on toys. See where he's lying? He loves to go into your room and lie on the carpet in that spot where the sunlight reaches the floor in the afternoon. I find him there nearly every day."

"He really is cute," Jojo commented. "I love his floppy ears."

"I'm really sorry he ruined your Lamby," Matt said.

Jojo thought back to that horrible day. It had hurt so much to lose the one thing that connected her to her daddy. She hugged her bear close as she realized that she hadn't really lost anything that day. Instead, she found a family. *If Boone hadn't destroyed Lamby, I wouldn't have my bear. I'm not sorry that happened.*

"Don't be sorry about Lamby," Jojo said. "I love that a part of my daddy will always be with me, but I also love that I have you and Amber and Eli, especially now. If this had happened when I was living with Miss Bonnie …" She couldn't even imagine how horrible that would have been. *She wouldn't have stayed here with me. She wouldn't have taken care of me. Thank you, Lord. Thank you for my family.*

Matt tightened his arm around her and kissed the top of her head. "So?" Matt asked. "Are you going to keep Boone?"

Jojo smiled and nodded. "Amber hasn't already promised him to someone else, has she?"

"No. Someone asked about him, but she was hoping you'd decide to keep him."

"I wish I could see him in person," Jojo said.

"I was just thinking about that," Matt said. "I don't think it would be wise to try to bring him here, especially with your counts so low right now. But I'll talk to Dr. O'Malley and see what he thinks. Hopefully you'll be able to come home before too much longer."

"I hope so," Jojo whispered as she rested her head on Matt's shoulder again. *I wish I knew if this chemo is even working. What if it isn't?* That thought made her shiver.

"Are you cold?" Matt asked, concern on his face.

"A little, I guess."

He got up and covered her with her purple blanket. Sitting beside her again, he touched her forehead with his hand. "You don't feel fevered to me, but we should have Brandon check just in case."

"They take my temperature every hour, I'm sure he'll be in soon."

"You're right. How's the prank war going? Has Brandon found a way to get you back for scaring him?"

Jojo giggled, "Yes! He came in to change my IV the other day. He was standing with his back to me while he did it. Then he turned around with this creepy old woman mask on. It made me jump then we both laughed."

"He's a funny guy," Matt said. "But he also seems to be very good at his job. I'm glad they take such good care of you."

"Everyone here is very nice," Jojo agreed. "Now I have to figure out how to get him back though."

"You should ask Eli for an idea. He's pulled off some pretty good pranks, that's for sure." Matt laughed, "He and Josh once snuck into his coach's office and wrapped the entire room in glittery Christmas wrapping paper. They covered the walls, ceiling, and chairs. Then they individually wrapped everything on his desk. Every pen, book, cup, everything."

Jojo laughed. "I would like to see pictures of that!"

"Thankfully their coach was a good sport. He thought it was hysterical."

A few moments later Brandon came in to check her temperature. "Oh," he said, "you have a bit of a fever. How are you feeling otherwise?"

"My head hurts, but that's all." *Oh no, does that mean I have an infection?* She looked at Matt to see if he seemed worried. He looked back at her and smiled a little. *He looks worried.*

"I'll let Dr. O'Malley know. We'll probably start you on an antibiotic in case you do have an infection. I'll be back in a few minutes," Brandon said and headed out the door.

"This is bad, isn't it?" Jojo whispered, wiping a tear from her cheek.

"Not necessarily," Matt said. "Let's get you back in bed." He helped her get situated and covered her with the purple blanket. "Remember what Dr. O'Malley said? He said that a fever can be caused by the chemo. It's not necessarily because of an infection. And they keep checking your temperature often so they can catch it early, which they did."

Matt pulled a chair close to her bed. Then, taking her small hand in his big one, he prayed for her again. While he prayed aloud,

Jojo prayed inside her head. *Lord, please help me!* When their prayer ended, Jojo took a deep breath. *What if this chemo doesn't work? The Bible says if I die, I'll go to Heaven. I know Heaven is supposed to be a great place, but it just sounds scary to me. I wonder if my daddy is there.*

Brandon did come back and give her an antibiotic. The whole time she tried to imagine what Heaven was like. She really didn't have any idea. *Maybe Matt knows. He studies the Bible all the time.*

After Brandon left, Matt stayed in the chair beside her bed. "Can I get you a drink or a snack or something?" he asked.

"No, thank you." She was suddenly nervous about asking Matt about Heaven, afraid she might not like his answer. She started picking at a piece of fuzz on her blanket. *Just ask him!* She finally worked up her courage and asked, "Matt, what's Heaven like?"

He looked at her for a moment. She couldn't tell what he was thinking, but then he smiled and answered, "Heaven is better than anything we have the ability to imagine."

"How do you know?"

"The Bible tells us a lot about it. There's much we don't know, but the things we do know are pretty awesome!"

"Like what? Do we all just float around on a cloud?"

He laughed. "No, it's much better than that! The Bible says that Heaven is a city, a very large city. We know the streets are made of gold. There is a tree that bears a different fruit every month. There is a river of very clear water. I think that God didn't tell us very much because we couldn't comprehend it. It's going to be more glorious than anything we have ever experienced on earth."

"That makes sense," Jojo commented. "When Annabeth tried to explain how amazing Hawaii is, I could sort of understand, but I probably don't have a very accurate picture in my mind."

"Exactly," Matt said, sounding pleased. "And you can see pictures of Hawaii and relate her description to things you are already familiar with. I think Heaven is so much greater than anything here that we don't have anything to compare it to in our minds."

"What will we do there, go to church all day?"

"Actually, there won't be any church buildings there. Think about it, we have churches here so we can worship and learn about God. We won't need that in Heaven. We will be in His actual presence. As for what we'll do, I don't know. I think we'll have things to do, but it will be work that we enjoy. It's really hard to say, I suppose."

Jojo thought about all that for a moment. Then she decided to ask the question she was most curious about. "Will my daddy be there? Will he recognize me?"

Matt sat back in his chair and looked Jojo in the eye. "Well, kiddo, I don't know for sure if he's in Heaven or not." Jojo looked away and picked at the fuzz on her blanket again. "Remember what the Bible says about how a person gets into Heaven?"

"Yes," she answered quietly. "If a person asks Jesus to be their Savior, they have eternal life in Heaven."

"Yes, you are exactly right." He gently touched the side of her face and made her look at him again. "Sweetheart, we don't know for sure if your daddy ever did that. But you said that he told you stories about going to church as a boy, right?"

She nodded.

"Then I'd say there's a very good chance your daddy did get saved as a boy. And, to answer your second question, he will definitely recognize you. The Bible tells us that."

Jojo took a deep breath and exhaled. Matt was right; there really was no way to know for sure, but she had every reason to believe her daddy was in Heaven waiting for her.

Matt smiled again. "Do you want to know some things that for sure will not be in Heaven?"

"Yes, what?" she asked.

"There will be no pain, no sickness, no sadness, no anger, no fear, no goodbyes. In fact, the Bible says that he will wipe away all our tears!"

Jojo smiled as she thought about that. *No more tears, that sounds wonderful.* She was starting to feel pretty sleepy, so she closed her eyes and tried to imagine what Heaven might look like.

Matt pulled the blanket up over Jojo's shoulders, making her feel nice and warm. Quietly he said, "You never have to be afraid because God is with you. He will never leave you."

Jojo opened her eyes and looked at Matt. "Heaven doesn't seem quite so scary now, but I still don't want to go there anytime soon."

"I don't want you to either," he said. "And, Jojo, I truly believe you are going to live a long and happy life. Dr. O'Malley says that everything that's happening right now is to be expected. Okay?"

"Okay," she agreed, blinking back a tear. "Thanks for taking care of me."

"You are so welcome, sweet girl." He stood and kissed her forehead. "Now, you need to get some sleep. Maybe you can dream up some way to get even with Brandon."

"Good idea," she said.

"I love you. Good-night."

"Good-night."

Lord, I do love my new family, but I'm afraid to tell them. They say they love me, and they show that they love me every day by the way they act. Still, I am so scared to trust this love is real. Will I ever be able to say what's in my heart?

CHAPTER 12

Thankfully they were able to continue as planned with Jojo's third chemo on Thursday. Even with the nausea medication, she felt pretty miserable for a few days. But by the following Tuesday, she was feeling more like herself. Her counts continued to stay low, so Matt, Amber, and Eli were her only visitors. That evening the four of them were enjoying dinner from Rowdy's. Jojo didn't have much of an appetite, but she managed to enjoy part of the delicious milkshake.

"Eli, I need to get even with Brandon for scaring me. Any ideas?" Jojo asked.

"Hmm, let me think. I have several Nerf guns and probably a thousand bullets at home. We could plan a surprise attack."

"Oh, that would be great!" Jojo said. "If you guys help me, we could get him from all sides."

Matt laughed. "I wonder what he'll come up with after this. You may end up regretting it."

"Never!" Jojo said confidently. "Can you bring them tomorrow? He said he works tomorrow and Thursday."

"He's coming," Amber said. She was standing near the door keeping watch. She had a nerf gun hidden behind her back. Jojo was sitting up in her bed with a nerf gun hidden under her purple blanket. Matt was sitting on a chair beside her bed, and Eli was on the couch. They each had loaded nerf guns ready as well.

As Brandon neared the door, Amber opened it for him. Jojo took the first shot and hit him on the arm. "Hey! Ouch!" Brandon said laughing. Then the barrage started. Jojo saw Amber hand Brandon her gun and pull out her cell phone to take pictures. Brandon aimed at Jojo, but she deflected the rubber tipped bullet with her blanket. Matt and Eli continued to shoot at Brandon, and he kept shooting at each of them until he was out of bullets. He stopped to reload and Jojo got him in the back of the head. He stepped closer and got her three times in a row.

She squealed and shot back in his direction. Unfortunately, she missed Brandon and hit Dr. O'Malley who was standing in the doorway shaking his head. Everyone froze for a second. "What's going on in here?" Dr. O'Malley said in a stern voice. He looked from one person to another. Then he added, "And why wasn't I invited?"

The room erupted in laughter as Matt handed Dr. O'Malley a nerf gun. He proceeded to shoot Brandon and Jojo. After a few joyful minutes, everyone settled down.

"I suppose I'd better get back to work before I lose my job," Brandon said. "I'll be back in a few minutes with your medicine. And, Jojo, just remember that I have a long memory." He laughed an evil-sounding laugh and left the room.

"I suppose I'd better get busy too," Dr. O'Malley said pulling a stool over to Jojo's bed. "I was going to ask how you're feeling, but I'm guessing pretty good."

Jojo smiled. "I do feel pretty good today. Not as achy."

"Well, how would you like to go home for a few days?"

"Seriously? I get to go home?"

"Your counts have come up some. You'll still need to be careful. No going out in public or anything, but I think you can go home and play with your puppy for a few days."

"Yes!" Jojo exclaimed. "I can't wait to see him! Can my friend Lylah visit?"

"I think that would be okay too." He looked at Matt and Amber. "Just be cautious of visitors who might be sick, but I think she should be fine." He turned back to Jojo. "Go home and enjoy that puppy, then we'll schedule your bone marrow biopsy for next week when you return. How does that sound?"

"Great! I can't wait to go home!"

They packed up all their belongings and waited around for Jojo to be discharged. A little before lunchtime, an orderly brought in a wheelchair to transport her to the car.

"I can walk," she reminded everyone, but Jason, the orderly, said that riding in a wheelchair was hospital policy.

Jojo had never been so happy to be outside in the sunshine. She grinned as the warm breeze tickled her face. They rode with the windows down and Jojo took off her hat, enjoying the feel of the wind on her head.

Matt turned the SUV onto Cardinal Street and Jojo could see the church and their house. Her heart began to beat faster. She was so excited to be home. She noticed that the church's parking lot was full of cars. "What's going on at church today?" she asked.

"Hmm," Matt said sounding unsure. "I have no idea."

As he turned into their driveway, a crowd of people suddenly flowed from their backyard and lined the driveway on both sides. Everyone cheered and waved, holding signs that said "Welcome

Home!" She saw Lylah and her family, Mr. John and Miss Evie, her Sunday school teacher, friends from school, and so many others.

Matt stopped the car and Mr. John approached his window. "Pastor Matt, we are so glad to have our girl home!" He turned to Jojo and said, "We sure have missed you!"

Jojo was speechless. Her heart felt as if it might beat right out of her chest. *He said "our girl".*

Mr. John continued, "We know you have to be super careful not to catch a sickness, so we won't get too close, and we won't stay long. You must be tired, but we just had to see you for a minute."

Jojo looked at Amber and saw she had tears running down her face. Then she realized she was crying herself. Matt looked as if he was feeling pretty emotional as well.

"Wow, thank you Mr. John. Thank you all," Matt said smiling at the crowd. "How about I pull into the garage and Jojo can come out on the porch and talk to you all for a few minutes?"

"If she feels up to it, that would be fine!" Mr. John answered.

They hurried into the house and were greeted by a very excited Ruthie and Boone. Jojo gave Ruthie a quick pat and scooped Boone up into her arms. He licked her face as she followed Matt and Amber out onto the front porch.

Matt moved three chairs to the edge of the porch and put Boone back inside the house because he wouldn't stop barking. They spent the next several minutes chatting with their church family. Many had brought gifts for Jojo and the family. Someone had even made them dinner.

Shortly the crowd of people began to say good-bye. Jojo couldn't believe how many people had come. Their smiles and well wishes made Jojo feel happy and special. *Lord, nobody ever much cared that I was around before I came here. Except for my daddy, I don't know if anybody else ever even loved me. But it's so different here. These people didn't have to come to see me today, but they did anyway.*

After everyone but Lylah and her family had left, they spent a few more minutes chatting. Matt let Ruthie and Boone back outside, and Jojo sat on the steps with Lylah cuddling the dogs and laughing. Jojo was feeling very tired again, but she tried not to let it show. She didn't want this time to end. Amber must have noticed because she said, "Lylah, are you free on Saturday? Jojo should have more energy by then. Maybe you could come and spend the day with her."

"Yes, I would love that!" Lylah said excitedly.

"I have an appointment at ten, I could drop her off a little before that," Lylah's dad offered.

"Perfect!" Amber said.

"We had better get going," Michelle said.

Lylah put Ruthie back down on the porch and hugged Jojo. "Bye! See ya Saturday! I'll text you later."

As they drove away, Amber said, "We have amazing friends. That was such a thoughtful surprise." Matt and Jojo both nodded in agreement. "But you are exhausted, Jojo. Let's get you inside so you can take a little nap."

Matt held out his hand to help her up.

"I don't want to go to sleep again," Jojo protested, but she still allowed Matt to help her to her feet. "All I do is sleep."

"Chemo is hard on your body. Try to remember this won't last forever," Matt reminded her. "Maybe if you climb in your bed Boone will take a snooze with you."

Boone did snuggle up beside her for a little while. She thought about how much he had grown in the weeks since she'd seen him last. Then, hearing Ruthie playing with a squeaking toy, he jumped off her bed and raced out the door. *He'll be as big as Ruthie before too long.* She thought about Matt's words: *"Try to remember this won't last forever." Lord, I know this won't last forever. Please let it end with me not dying from this leukemia.*

On Saturday morning, Jojo was not feeling very well. She was really looking forward to spending the day with Lylah, and she had been sure she would have more energy by now. But, for some reason, she was achy and tired. She sat at the kitchen table while Amber made breakfast. Part of her just wanted to go back to bed, but she couldn't stand the thought of missing out on a fun day with Lylah. Amber turned from the stove and watched Jojo for moment, then asked, "Are you sure you're feeling up to company today?"

"How do you always know when I don't feel good?" Jojo asked.

Amber smiled and walked over to place her hand on Jojo's forehead. "I can see it in your eyes. When you are feeling good, your eyes twinkle. You don't seem to have a fever, but I'll have to get the thermometer to be sure."

"I'll be fine," Jojo responded. "I am really excited for Lylah to come over."

"I know you are." Amber returned to the stove and flipped a pancake. "Let's see how the morning goes. Lylah will understand if I need to drive her home early."

"Okay." Jojo felt bad enough that she didn't even argue about possibly cutting her fun day short.

Lylah arrived just as Jojo was finishing breakfast. Amber suggested the girls enjoy the porch swing while they chatted. Jojo realized Amber was trying to help her have a good time without doing an activity that would require a lot of energy. *She takes such good care of me.*

Things went well for a while, but then Jojo started feeling really sleepy. She tried to hide it from Lylah, but it didn't work. Lylah was telling Jojo all about the end of the year school picnic when she started nodding off.

Lylah was offended. "Jojo!" she said in an annoyed voice. "I thought you wanted to talk. You've hardly said two words this whole time. Now, you're falling asleep!" She huffed and crossed her arms across her chest. "Do you not want me to be here?"

Jojo gasped, "No! I mean, yes! I do want you here." She wiped a tear from her eye and tried to explain, "I'm sorry. I'm just really tired today. Some days I have lots of energy, and some days I don't."

Lylah looked as if she wasn't sure what to say. Finally, she said, "It's okay. It's not your fault you're sick. Maybe I should call my mom to come and get me."

"Please don't leave yet," Jojo pleaded. "It's almost lunch time. Please stay for lunch at least."

"Okay, if you're sure you're up to it," Lylah said.

"I am!" Jojo sat up straight and concentrated on paying attention to the things Lylah was saying.

Amber had invited Michelle to join them for lunch and had brought home Rowdy's burgers and milkshakes for them. The meal was delicious, but Jojo was relieved when Michelle and Lylah finally left. As soon as the door closed behind them, she headed to her bed.

Amber followed her and covered her with a blanket. She sat on the edge of the bed and wiped a tear from Jojo's cheek. "I'm sorry your day wasn't what you had planned."

"Me too. I'm so tired of being sick."

"I know you are. And actually, I am too." Amber giggled. "I can't wait for you to really feel better so we can go shopping together!"

"That sounds nice," Jojo whispered. "I like spending time with you."

"I'm so glad!" Amber said. "I like spending time with you too! As a matter of fact, I think you and I need to plan a special trip as soon as your treatments are over. Think about where you'd like to go. We could even go somewhere for a whole weekend."

"Really?" Jojo asked. "It would be like a real vacation?"

"Yes, a mini-vacation."

"I've never been on an actual vacation before."

"You haven't?" Amber said, sounding a little surprised. "Then we'll have to talk to Matt and Eli and plan a family vacation for next summer. Maybe the beach! Would you like that?"

"I've never been to a beach, but I've always wanted to see the ocean and put my feet in the sand!"

"You will love it! For now though, you need to get some rest. That's the best thing for your body right now."

Boone seemed to sense that something wasn't right with Jojo. He came into her room and whined until Amber lifted him up on the bed. He tilted his head sideways and looked at Jojo. Then, with a whine, he began licking her face. She giggled and wrapped her arms around him. Finally, he settled in beside her and sighed.

After Amber left her room, Jojo thought about all the fun things Amber had just mentioned. *It really is like a real family! Thank you, Lord. Please let this chemo be working! Please help me to get better soon and help my adoption to work out. I never want to leave here.*

CHAPTER 13

Sunday evening, they returned to the hospital. She was admitted to the exact same room as before. As much as Jojo didn't want to be there, she was glad that she would soon know if the chemo was working. That night, after everything settled down and the lights were out, Jojo had trouble falling asleep. She couldn't help but think about the possibility that the chemo wasn't working. *If this doesn't work, I might die. I just got a new family, and I might lose them. God, please, please, please let the leukemia be gone. Please!*

She remembered the Bible verse Amber had taught her. "What time I am afraid, I will trust in Thee." *Please help me not to be afraid. I'm trying really hard to trust you.*

She closed her eyes and eventually fell asleep. Emily woke her very early the next morning to go have the bone marrow biopsy. Jojo didn't remember any of it, but she was thankful for the Tylenol they gave her that afternoon. Other than some soreness in her back, she was feeling pretty well.

School was out for the summer, and with the help of her teachers and family, Jojo had finished the year with all A's. Now, being confined to her room with only her family to visit, and with all her schoolwork finished, Jojo was very restless. The rest of the day seemed to last forever.

Monday afternoon there was still no word on the biopsy results. Jojo's anxiety over the possible results was making the time pass even more slowly. She felt quite grouchy. So, when Amber asked her what she wanted for dinner, Jojo answered with a rude, "Nothing."

She immediately realized how she sounded and thought she ought to apologize. But, instead of apologizing, she said, "Why can't you just leave me alone? I'm not hungry, but you're always trying to make me eat something."

Surprisingly, Amber didn't say anything about Jojo's stinky attitude. Instead, she said, "Then why don't you try to take a little nap? You were awake pretty early this morning."

"I'm sick of sleeping. I'm sick of eating. I'm sick of this room. I'm sick of everything." Jojo retorted.

"You're not the only one," Amber agreed quietly.

The rest of the evening passed much the same way. Jojo just couldn't seem to get her feelings or her words under control. She knew she was being mean to Amber, but she couldn't make herself stop. *Where are those results? This is torture! I need to know if the chemo's working!*

She tried to think about other things to keep her mind occupied, but everything seemed to make her think of them. She looked out the window and saw cars moving in the parking lot below. *Will I live long enough to get to drive?*

She picked up her phone to text Lylah. *If I die, who will help her with math?*

She pulled the bag of orange gumdrops out of her bag and ate the last three. *What if those were my last orange gumdrops ever?*

She sat on the edge of her bed and hugged her bear. *Will I live long enough to get adopted?*

Through the open bathroom door, Jojo could see Amber standing at the sink brushing her teeth. She thought about all the fun things Amber had done with her in the few months that she'd lived with them. She remembered watching Ruthie having the puppies, planting flowers, baking brownies, going shopping, playing games, and watching movies. *Will I ever get to do those things with her again? Will I get to go on that weekend trip with her, or a family vacation to the beach?*

Jojo's eyes stung with tears. She climbed under the covers and pretended to be asleep. She didn't want to talk to Amber, she just wanted this night to be over. She wanted to know one way or the other if the chemo was working.

She kept her eyes closed and listened as Amber quietly prepared for bed. She felt Amber gently kiss her forehead as she whispered, "Good-night, sweet girl."

Finally, the room was dark and Jojo let the silent tears fall. *Please, God! Please let the results come back soon!*

Sometime later Jojo could tell by the sound of her breathing that Amber was asleep. She listened to the muffled sounds of the hospital. She could hear the helicopter coming near and knew it would be landing on the roof. Emily had explained that it flew critical patients to the hospital when the situation was so bad that they couldn't be transported by ambulance fast enough.

She heard a baby crying from somewhere down the hall. She was so used to the various beeps from equipment, that she hardly ever noticed them anymore. Occasionally she would hear a voice outside her room. At night, she could almost always identify the person to whom the voice belonged. She recognized most of the staff members and the patients who were in the rooms near hers.

The nurses were very good about trying not to wake sleeping patients if they didn't have to. Jojo knew that they frequently took her temperature throughout the night, but most of the time she slept right through it.

Brandon quietly opened her door and came over to check her. He smiled and whispered, "What are you still doing awake?"

"Can't sleep," she whispered back.

"Your temperature is normal. You'd better try to get some rest."

"Good-night."

He walked into the little room with the sink and closed the door. Jojo could still hear him standing on the other side of the door, typing on his computer, and talking on the phone to someone.

"Yes, Doctor, I saw the report. No, it wasn't good …" Brandon's voice stopped as he apparently listened to the voice on the phone. "What time should I tell them to expect you?... Okay, I'll take care of it."

Jojo couldn't listen to anymore. She buried her face in her pillow. *The report is bad? That means the chemo isn't working!* Quiet sobs shook her whole body. Even though she knew this was a possibility, she was still shocked to hear those actual words. *"I saw the report. No, it wasn't good."*

God, help! How can the chemo not be working? What am I going to do?

"What time I am afraid, I will trust in Thee."

I'm trying to trust you.

Suddenly Amber wrapped her arms around Jojo and pulled her up. She rocked her back and forth. "What's wrong, sweetheart?"

Jojo tried to explain, but all she could say was, "I'm dying."

Amber held her tightly, "No, Jojo, you're fine. We're in the hospital and they're giving you chemo to get rid of the leukemia."

Jojo continued to cry. "You don't understand," she sobbed. "I heard Brandon say the report is back and the chemo isn't working. I don't want to die alone! Will you stay with me?" Jojo pleaded.

"Jojo," Amber said as she stopped rocking and placed her hands on the sides of Jojo's face. Looking into her eyes, Amber promised, "I will not leave you alone. I promise!"

"Okay." Jojo felt a tiny bit of relief.

"But, sweetheart, maybe you didn't hear what you thought you heard."

"I heard Brandon say, 'Yes, Doctor, I saw the report. No, it wasn't good …'"

"Well, let's not jump to conclusions. I'll ask him to come in and we'll find out what's going on."

"But Amber, what if I am really dying?"

Amber wrapped her arms around Jojo and started rocking again. "Remember that talk you had with Matt about Heaven?"

Jojo nodded.

"If you really are dying, you'll get to go there before the rest of us. It's a wonderful place."

"I'm just so scared."

"God knows what's best for us, even better than we do. So, we need to trust him to do what's best. He tells us not to worry, but to make our requests to him. And he will give us a peace which passes all understanding. Let's pray and ask him to give us that peace."

While Amber prayed aloud, Jojo prayed silently. *Dear Jesus, you know that I'm so afraid. I do not want to die yet! But I know that if I do, I'll get to go to Heaven with you. Help me to trust you and help me to not be afraid. Please give me peace. Amen.*

After they finished praying, Amber turned on the light and handed Jojo a tissue. They both wiped their tears and took a deep breath. "It's all going to be okay," Amber said as she squeezed Jojo's hand. "I don't know what the future holds, but I know we can trust the One who holds your future."

"I know," Jojo agreed. "I can't explain it. I'm still scared, but I feel better, calmer, somehow. I'm scared of what might be coming, but yet, I believe Heaven will be wonderful."

"And," Amber added, "I just remembered what Dr. O'Malley said in the beginning. He said that if this chemo isn't working like we'd hoped, there are still many other options. So, even if this report is bad, it doesn't mean you're going to die."

Jojo smiled, "I forgot he said that. I've been so worried about this report, but I guess it might not be as bad as I thought."

"Exactly!" Amber squeezed her hand again. "I'm going to see if Brandon is in the hall. I'll be right back."

A few moments later Brandon and Amber came into the room. Jojo could tell by the smile on Amber's face that they had good news.

"I'm really sorry to have scared you, Jojo," Brandon said. "I was talking to Dr. Mills about a staff report."

Relief flooded through Jojo. *Maybe everything's going to be okay.*

"Your biopsy report did come in about twenty minutes ago and it looks like everything is going just like we hoped."

Oh, thank you, Lord!

"I'm not a doctor, so I really can't say much more than that, but Dr. O'Malley will be in first thing in the morning to go over the results with you. But don't you worry, kiddo. Everything looks good."

Brandon left and Amber turned off the light. "Will you lie with me until I fall asleep?" Jojo asked.

Amber smiled and lay down beside her. She wrapped her arm around Jojo and whispered, "I love you, Jojo."

"I love you too," Jojo whispered back. "I'm so happy that I get to have you for a mom."

Amber squeezed her tight and said, "Me too!"

The next morning, Dr. O'Malley confirmed what Brandon had said. The chemo was doing exactly what they had hoped. He explained that Jojo still had a long road ahead of her, but there was every reason to expect she would make a full recovery. Jojo couldn't remember a time in her life when she had ever felt this happy.

For the first time since my daddy died, I feel like everything's going to be okay! Thank you, Lord! Thank you for letting this chemo work, and for giving me a family!

EPILOGUE

Six months later the Morrises were getting ready to celebrate. It was Thanksgiving Day and Jojo was in the kitchen helping Amber and Eli prepare dinner. Ruthie and Boone were lying on a rug by the door, waiting for crumbs to fall on the floor. Jojo's last chemo treatment was over, and she was officially cancer-free. Of course, her doctors would continue to monitor her for the next several years, but everyone was hopeful that it would never return.

School was going well so far. She was doing everything online, and her teachers had been very helpful. At Dr. O'Malley's recommendation, it was decided that Jojo would not return to school in person until after Christmas. He wanted to make sure her blood count had time to go up before she spent a lot of time in public where she would be exposed to all the usual sicknesses that pass through a school each year.

"These smell delicious! Jojo, it looks like your first attempt at making pies is a success," Amber commented as she lifted two pumpkin pies out of the oven.

"I think you'd better wait until we taste them before you say that, Mom," Eli said as he lifted the pan holding the turkey and slid it into the oven. "How long does this thing take to bake?"

"It weighs about twelve pounds, so only about three hours. The desserts are finished, so we can take a break for a while. Then we'll come back and get everything else ready. I told your dad we'd eat about four o'clock," Amber answered.

"I wonder what's taking him so long," Jojo commented. "I thought he'd be home by now. He said we'd play a game of football in the backyard this afternoon."

"I thought you hated football," Eli said.

"I used to. But we used to watch games on TV when I was in the hospital sometimes. I guess I finally started liking it." Jojo shrugged. "Besides, actually playing a game is always more fun than watching it, especially if Dad plays."

"I don't know what's keeping him," Amber said. "He was just making a quick visit to Mr. Bailey. The man is ninety years old and doesn't have any family who lives around here. He's been in the hospital for weeks and is feeling pretty lonely. I'm sure he'll be here soon."

Just then, as if he knew they were talking about him, Matt opened the door and came into the kitchen. "Happy Thanksgiving!" he exclaimed.

"Happy Thanksgiving!" they all said in return.

"It sure smells good in here. Is it dinnertime yet?"

"Uh, not quite yet," Jojo said with a smile. "We have time to play a game of football first."

"Yes! You're on my team. Eli, your mom's not very good. Sorry!" Matt teased.

"Hey!" Amber said, sounding offended. "You might be surprised!"

"Before we go outside, I have to give Jojo something. I stopped by Mr. John's house on the way home from the hospital. Mr. John made this for you." He handed Jojo a little green gift bag with a red bow. "He knew we'd be going to get a Christmas tree tomorrow and wanted you to have this before then."

Jojo opened the bag and found a wooden Christmas ornament with four snowmen painted on it. Printed on the top were the words "The Morris Family". Then their first names were printed underneath the four snowmen. It was beautiful. "I love it!"

"There's one more thing," Amber said. "I know I promised you a trip to the beach when your treatments were finished, and we will do that. But we thought you might enjoy going on a family vacation now to celebrate your adoption being final. So, on Monday we are all going to Snowshoe Mountain Resort to go skiing!"

"Seriously?" Jojo asked. "Thank you, Mom!"

"Well it was my idea," Matt said with a pretend frown.

"Thank you too, Dad!" Jojo said as she hugged them both.

"Since this was originally supposed to be a girl's trip, I booked a day at the spa for just me and you while we're there," Amber added.

"I can't believe this! I'm so excited! There's just one problem though. I don't know how to ski."

"We'll teach you," Eli said. "I've seen how determined you are. You'll learn fast. We can go snowboarding and tubing there too."

"Don't worry, Jojo. I'm sure it will be fine," Matt said with a wink. "Now let's get this game started!" He rubbed the top of her head. "Hey, you've got some hair growing back already."

Jojo rubbed the top of her own head and felt the soft downy growth. "I do! I hadn't even noticed." She grinned at Amber. "It's like you said—hair always grows back!"

ABOUT THE AUTHOR

Angela Tanner has a BA in elementary education and has taught middle-grade children in Christian schools for twenty-five years. She studied children's literature and writing at the Institute of Children's Literature and completed the registered instructor program from the Institute for Excellence in Writing. Her article "Effective Review Games" was recently published in the Journal for Christian Educators. Angela lives with her family in West Virginia.

Made in United States
Orlando, FL
18 April 2023

32198295R10085